LORE

I live in Wiltshire with have lived in four continents. From playing amidst Roman ruins in Africa as a child to riding a Sultan's racehorse in the Middle East as a teen, I've many experiences to draw on for the stories I've been writing ever since I can remember. When I'm not writing you'll find me listening to audiobooks while I sew or design handbags, usually with a rescue terrier or two curled up on my feet!

Confessions
of a Chalet Girl

LORRAINE WILSON

Harper*Impulse* an imprint of
HarperCollins*Publishers Ltd*
77–85 Fulham Palace Road
Hammersmith, London W6 8JB

www.harpercollins.co.uk

A Paperback Original 2014

First published in Great Britain in ebook format by HarperImpulse 2013

Cover Images © Shutterstock.com

Lorraine Wilson asserts the moral right to
be identified as the author of this work

A catalogue record for this book
is available from the British Library

ISBN: 9780007559572

This novel is entirely a work of fiction.
The names, characters and incidents portrayed in it are
the work of the author's imagination. Any resemblance to
actual persons, living or dead, events or localities is
entirely coincidental.

Automatically produced by Atomik ePublisher from Easypress

For the Minxes of Romance, Jackie Ashenden, Charlotte Phillips and Heidi Rice – without your encouragement to keep writing this book wouldn't exist. Thank you!

CHAPTER ONE

'Get it off!'

Shouts and wolf whistles filled the packed bar. Embarrassment prickled at Holly Buchanan's skin. Chalet girl initiation huh? Why not just throw her to the lions and have done with it?

Swallowing hard, she scanned the crowd. Could she pull this off? They looked inebriated enough to have their designer wool scarves pulled over their eyes.

Bras of all colours and sizes dangled from the wooden beams of the bar's ceiling, resembling pastel-coloured Christmas decorations. 'The Wonderbar', the venue for her first night out in Verbier was, despite appearances, not a seedy strip joint but a favourite haunt of savvy seasonnaires. Not to mention the occasional billionaire.

She heard it grew pretty steamy in the small hours. Not that she was planning on sticking around to see. No way was she dancing on a table.

A throbbing tension headache pulsated against her temples.

What the frick am I doing here?

Enduring ritual humiliation in return for the ten free shots her team would get if she whipped off her bra was hardly her idea of a good night out.

'Off, off, off.'

Her heart performed a neat back flip down to the soles of her boots.

Come on Holly, work it! You can do it.

'Off, off, off.'

She took a deep breath and stepped forward. It wasn't as if she even wanted the blasted drinks but failure was not an option. Fitting in was going to be difficult. Her wavy auburn hair contrasted with the straight, identikit caramel locks of the other chalet girls and a glimpse in the mirror confirmed she was paler than an anemic ghost beside their healthy tans. She'd packed for winter, not clubbing, and her cheap cashmere sweater clashed with the other chalet girls' strappy, sparkly tops that defied the sub-zero temperatures outside.

'Off, off, off,' the chanting grew louder and more impatient.

I hate, hate, hate this…

She slid one hand up underneath her jumper, giving silent thanks to veteran chalet girl Sophie who'd warned her about the initiation. It'd given her time to come up with a miraculous idea. An idea that had to work because no way was she doing this for real.

'Off... Off... Off…'

'Okay, okay. Give me a sec.' She hoped she sounded breezy, fun…

Fun.

If she heard that word once more she swore she'd walk out into the snow and pray for an avalanche.

'It's a girl's prerogative to take her time,' she said her line, attempting a false flirty smile while she pretended to be fiddling with her bra straps. Face burning with embarrassment, she pulled out the second bra she'd secreted inside the sweater before she left the chalet. A barman then snatched it out of her hands and hooked the strap over a nail on the beam. Raucous cheers were mixed with muttered complaints she hadn't flashed the crowd.

As if!

Sophie emerged from the scrum at the bar, her tanned face lit up with an enormous grin. She handed a shot glass to Holly. 'A toast to you Holly. You're officially one of us.'

2

Holly smiled and took the glass, even though she wasn't sure she'd be able to stomach it. At least the ordeal was over. The alcohol burned her throat and comforting warmth spread through her chest as she gazed around the bar at the spectators she hadn't dared to make eye contact with so far.

The bar was packed with seasonnaires – chalet girls and ski or snowboard instructors starting the winter season as they meant to continue. Holly wished for the umpteenth time, with a gut-churning wrench, that her flatmate Pippa were here. This job had been all her idea when last winter's dreary London drizzle had seemed unending. She'd chosen the resort because an online review had voted it 'best resort for anyone looking to marry rich'. Pippa's eyes lit up as she read aloud to Holly tales of £5,000-a-pop cocktails and the celebs and royalty who graced the resort, landing at the nearby airfield in their private jets.

How ironic that Pippa had fallen in love with penniless mechanic Steve, fallen pregnant and moved him into their rented flat in Wimbledon, leaving Holly with the option of taking the Verbier job as planned or going back home. At this very moment her room in the flat was being converted into a nursery.

Going back home was not an option. Getting a peek into the world of the rich and famous seemed an enticing prospect, like stepping into the pages of a magazine. Not that she could spot anyone famous tonight. Although…

Her eyes came to an abrupt halt as they met the interested gaze of a man with broad, rugby player shoulders and the confident stance of someone completely at ease with himself. He stood head and shoulders above some of the young ski instructors at his side. He was easily handsome enough to be an actor but his dark hair was too mussed and his face too weathered for someone who cared overly about his looks.

Minor royalty perhaps? Or maybe a Russian oligarch? He certainly had the arrogance of one. He stared at her unashamedly, the corners of his mouth twitching with amusement. Looking up at the latest addition to the bras swinging from the beam overhead he raised an eyebrow.

'Not yours,' he mouthed, a crinkle of a smile stretching across a tanned face shadowed by evening stubble.

Oh really? Who did this smart-alec think he was? He might act like a prince but most likely he was just a ski-slob instructor looking to make her another notch on his ski pole.

Emboldened by adrenaline from her 'initiation' and the heady warmth radiating though her body from the Schnapps, she negotiated the crowded bar to get to him.

She couldn't let him mouth off about her not doing the initiation properly. What if they made her do it again? For real next time? She had to shut him up.

'Hi, I'm Holly,' she introduced herself coolly, mimicking his raised eyebrows. 'Who are you?'

Perhaps the ice in her voice would cool his over-familiarity?

'Scott.' He surprised her by offering his hand to shake, an oddly formal gesture for his jeans and T-shirt, laid back vibe. Instinctively she took it, his warm hand engulfing hers, clasping it for slightly longer than necessary.

Nice hands.

Involuntarily she found her gaze lingering on his toned physique. Her frostiness hadn't brought the temperature down one iota and her icy attitude lay in a puddle around her feet. A strange prickle tickled her skin, not embarrassment this time but something even more unwelcome – desire.

I'm supposed to be confronting him, not offering myself on a plate!

Hastily stealing her hand back, she vowed to resist his charm and chemistry, all six foot two inches of it.

Who was this man? Given he was fit and bronzed by sun and wind, he should have blended easily into the crowd. Yet something about the confident way he held himself and his effortless self-possession set him apart.

'I guess this isn't your first season in Verbier, Scott?' She tried to

4

keep her tone neutral, to ignore the buzz of anticipation building inside her. Her body registered the off the scale attraction, desire tugging at her mind for attention.

Could I? Maybe?

Everywhere in the crowd couples were discreetly, or not so discreetly, pairing off. This was too quick though. She couldn't just hook up with the first gorgeous guy she met. She knew nothing about him.

I don't do this kind of thing.

Scott stared at her with interested amusement, as though reading her mind. Her cheeks grew hot. She was aware, too aware of the warmth of his body temptingly close to her and the faintest hint of Armani Mania, her favourite aftershave. Time to make an exit. Armani Mania was worse than cocktails for appealing to her most primal instincts.

'It's not exactly my first season, no,' Scott answered her, still staring with naked curiosity. Like he was trying to solve a complex puzzle. The corners of his lips twitched with ill concealed humour.

Holly folded her arms over her chest; instinctively aware she'd made a faux pas. Heat spread from her cheeks to her neck. She hated looking stupid. Possibly as much as she loathed crowds of people watching her take her underwear off in public.

'Hey!' Sophie bumped into her back in the crush. She rested a hand on Holly's shoulder and whispered into her ear, her breath reeking of schnapps. 'He's our boss you muppet! Lay off the seduction routine, he hates it, won't sleep with the staff… unfortunately.'

Was it Holly's imagination or had the chatter in the bar quietened at that very moment? It always seemed to when you didn't want someone to hear, it was one of those immutable laws like toast landing butter side down.

Scott's eyes gleamed, they really did look black. Although on closer inspection his irises contained flecks of dark brown, a deep cafe noir. His lips twitched again as he suppressed a smile. He'd heard every word.

'I'm not, I wasn't…' she muttered, shooting a furious glance at Sophie who raised her eyebrows and disappeared back into the crowd.

Oh great. Fan-bloody-tastic!

'Nice to meet you, Mr. Hamilton.' She bit back her surprise that he was the owner of Luxury Chalet Experiences. He was… different to how she'd imagined. Much more of an athlete than a suit.

'It's okay. You can call me Scott.' He grinned and Holly felt unwittingly caught up in his smile, like a fly in a spider's web. She bathed in the warmth of it, transfixed. Her gaze travelled over his long, muscled limbs. He must be really fit…

Stop this at once Holly!

Mentally she shook her head, hoping to break his spell.

'Can I get you a drink?' He gestured towards her glass.

'I've already got one.' She clutched the shot glass to her chest, trying to conceal the fact it was empty.

Why did people always try to force alcohol on you? She'd never get how losing control was equated with having a good time. Holly never got drunk. Mum had cured her of any desire to have one drink too many.

'Ah yes, the Schnapps was your reward for the 'performance' you put on tonight. I didn't realise I paid my staff so little they had to strip to make an extra buck.'

Taken aback, she narrowed her eyes, seething and biting back the retort that après-ski activities had certainly not been specified in her job description.

Being leered at by a group of trust fund ski bums wasn't her life's ambition. She was here to see Switzerland, to learn to ski, to maybe have an adventure… She didn't know what sort of adventure but it certainly wouldn't involve getting legless in a bar adorned with girls' underwear.

She shrugged, wishing a witty retort would come to mind. She'd think of it later tonight no doubt but for now her mind was peculiarly absent, still ruminating on the long denim-clad legs and strong arms. Not to mention that gorgeous whiff of Armani Mania playing havoc with her senses.

Get real, Holly.

'Just kidding.' His mouth widened into another grin. 'I don't mind my staff having fun, as long as their hangovers don't keep them from making the breakfasts first thing in the morning. And you were certainly playing to the audience.'

What was that supposed to mean? She crossed her arms over her chest. Fun! Huh. Now where was an avalanche when you needed one?

After a five am start this morning to get to Luton airport in time for her flight to Geneva she really could be doing without this. The familiar signs of growing drunkenness around her increased her discomfort.

Gorgeous or not she wanted out of here.

Oh to escape to bed and pull the duvet up over her head away from prying eyes. She wondered how he'd known it wasn't her real bra. She glanced involuntarily up at the plain white bra dangling from the beam. Scott caught her eye and winked.

'I think I'll go back to the chalet. I've got a call to make and I was planning on an early night.' She spoke to the floorboards, heat flooding her cheeks. It would be a relief to get outside in the cold night air.

'Good plan. You've a seven am start tomorrow morning to help get Chalet Repos ready for the new guests.'

She had to get out of here before she embarrassed herself even more.

'I'll, err, make that call.' She hurriedly fished her iPhone out of her jeans pocket. 'I'm going to head off now, the signal here's rubbish.'

'I'll come with you.' He took her empty glass from her and placed it on a table. 'I've got some paperwork to do. And we need to sort your ski-pass. Sorry I wasn't around earlier but driving back from Italy was hellish – the passes were shut because of this early snowfall so I had to drive the long way round. But Sophie looked after you, right?'

Disconcerted, Holly had no choice but to let him join her. She felt in the wrong, a sulky teenager being handled patiently by the teacher.

'Yes, she was really helpful,' she said, staring down at her boots while he pulled his jacket on. She should be summoning a party girl smile and exuding some of that 'can-do' attitude she'd performed so well at the agency interview back in London. Heck, she'd even convinced herself at the time!

She ignored Sophie's smirk as they left the bar together, their footsteps crunching into the crisp, compacted snow. A new layer of powdery snow had fallen since she'd arrived at the Wonderbar. The reflected moonlight sparkled like diamonds on the snow's surface.

It was quiet, positively serene. A polar opposite to the bar. She couldn't deny the resort was beautiful. Really she should make the most of it, stop being stroppy. She'd chosen to come here after all.

'Who are you ringing?

In the silent, deserted street Scott's voice felt intimate. His breath evaporated on the freezing air. Holly looked down at the snow, flummoxed. 'I have to ring a friend, my flatmate Pippa. She was supposed to be here with me but she… um got pregnant.'

Great Holly, way to make an impression!

'You were happy to come on your own though?'

Hot, unexpected tears burned at the back of her eyes. She blinked them back, feeling the muscles in her neck tensing. She shrugged. 'Sure. Why not? It'll be an experience.'

'You don't mind being away from your family for Christmas and New Year?'

'No,' she said, ignoring the urge to tell him the truth about why she'd been so keen to come here. The idea of going home for Christmas was so unpalatable she'd have gone to a Siberian work camp if it had been the only option on offer.

'You're lucky your family don't mind you being away.' His jaw tightened, a shuttered look briefly obscuring his features.

She snorted. 'They don't mind, no. So you don't have a choice?'

'Nope, I've got to fly back to London, act as referee, make sure no one actually kills anyone.' He sighed and kicked at the snow. 'Frankly I'd rather stay here and work.'

'It doesn't sound much fun.' She grimaced in sympathy but didn't want to delve deeper. Confidences invited confidences and she couldn't go there.

Her mother and her new partner would spend Christmas blind drunk. It might be all right for a while, until the rowing started. A shiver ran down her spine and she hugged her arms around her body, head pounding.

'Here.' Scott took his ski jacket off and put it over her shoulders.

The warmth enveloped her like a hug and tears threatened again. She blinked them back fiercely.

Don't be nice to me, just don't.

'You need to be careful out here in the cold.' Scott frowned. If he'd seen her glistening eyes he chose not to mention it. 'The temperatures at night can be dangerously low. Barely a season goes by without a drunken tourist having to be fished out of the frozen river in the morning. The ice is treacherous. You girls need to take more care. Particularly if you're drinking shots.'

You girls?

She glared at him. How dare he give her a lecture about alcohol? As if she hadn't grown up with the consequences, had them thrust in her face every day…

Ok this was good. Being angry she could handle. So there were a few chemical reactions happening between them. The guy had good pheromones. So what? Nothing would happen.

You need to take more care.

She did nothing *but* bloody well take care. As soon as she was old enough she was cleaning up vomit, encouraging her mother to change, to wash her hair, to maintain the semblance of a normal home for all the prying eyes and snoops. Terror at the idea of being put into care meant she perfected the art of pretending everything

9

was okay. Then the years trying to get her mother to AA meetings before the gut-wrenching conclusion she never would because she simply didn't want to.

'Right,' she replied, voice tight and her throat aching with the words she wasn't saying. Her heart felt as cold and heavy as the patches of thick ice on the path. She didn't want his advice, didn't want his... Well, maybe she did want his jacket. It was bloody freezing after all.

'Are you okay?' The warmth in his tone and the absence of a mocking, teasing air made her almost think about confiding.

Almost.

'I'm fine thanks, really pleased to be here.' She smiled a tight smile. 'Thanks for giving me the opportunity to work here.'

Fine, so she deserved the raised eyebrow she got for that, it sounded insincere even to her own ears. She met his gaze levelly, defiantly, flashing a 'no entry' sign as politely as she knew how.

It was a look she'd practiced and used to great effect with teachers prying into her home life when she was a child and she'd carried it on into adulthood. It had been a useful tool in her defence arsenal.

'I'm thinking you don't normally get to have much fun, Holly.' The flirty edge was back in his voice and a spark danced in his eyes. Clearly she needed to practice her 'piss-off look'. Either that or he was immune. That was a scary thought.

'Fun?' She ground her teeth, immensely grateful they were almost at the chalet.

'Yes, you know. That thing where you relax, let your guard down, lose control.'

'I never lose control,' she replied, pulling his jacket more tightly around her body.

The snow-covered porch of Chalet Repos was a welcome sight. She huddled in the doorway as he pulled out his keys to let them into the basement staff quarters.

'That sounds like a challenge,' he said. His eyes locked on hers with an intensity that was dark and probing, seeing… what? Far too much, anyway.

She couldn't look away, the connection between them mesmerising her, accompanied by a tug of desire so visceral it took her breath away.

Flakes of snow fell, softly tickling her nose and resting on her eyelashes.

'It's snowing again.' She broke away first, stamping her boots on the doormat to dislodge the snow.

Scott laughed and turned the key in the lock. 'Call that snow? Just you wait until we get the really heavy falls. Oh, I meant to ask you – whose was the bra you pretended to remove?'

The change of subject startled her. She stared at him, flushing again as something knowing and very, very sexy flashed in his dark eyes.

He held the door open and she slipped past him, the warmth of the chalet enveloped her as she stepped inside, senses tingling and skin super sensitised. His hand lightly brushed her arm when he took his jacket back. She started violently. Had he done that on purpose?

'Err, what makes you so sure it wasn't mine?' The words escaped her mouth before she could stop them. Never ask a question you don't want the answer to.

Too late.

CHAPTER TWO

Scott couldn't help but grin. Holly intrigued him. He knew he should maintain a professional distance but what the hell, it was fun playing with her. She was a puzzle to be solved, a challenge to rise to. On the surface she seemed to be acting a part, that line about being grateful for the opportunity had been falser than her little strip routine.

Usually he hated that kind of superficiality but her eyes had a depth and intelligence that blew him away. Intuition told him there was more to her than met the eye, although he had to admit what met the eye – the lush curves of her body and wavy auburn hair – was an absolute treat.

Clearly all was not well back home. Well he could certainly relate to that.

Generally the chalet girls the agency sent him were a hardy breed who partied like it was their vocation. They worked efficiently enough so they could get maximum time on the ski slopes and in the bars at night. Some were looking for flings, others looking for rings.

Holly didn't fit the Hooray Henrietta mould.

Nor did she fit the bra she'd so carefully tried to pass off as her own.

'It was too small,' he replied bluntly, trying not to laugh too openly, watching the deepening flush of her cheeks. She was so

12

easy to tease. Making her blush was hardly a challenge. He liked it that Holly was sweet but also very, very sexy.

Holly crossed her arms over her chest and glowered at him, but tellingly her pupils dilated into two black pools, vivid against irises of deep forest green. Her lips parted.

He knew the signs when a woman was attracted to him. But this felt different. More. Warmer, softer and far more meaningful.

He should lay off, take a step back.

She's staff, remember!

A glimpse of pink tongue between Holly's white teeth distracted him and he wondered how she would taste if he kissed her. This was all her fault for being so damned irresistible.

'The bra was too plain as well. I'm guessing you're a lacy bra kind of girl, and you go in for colour too.'

'Oh.' Her mouth opened and then abruptly closed again as she fixed her eyes on her boots. Her body might be speaking the language of desire but her troubled eyes said she was conflicted.

Scott regretfully decided it was time to back off. Time to act like an employer.

Remember what happened last time you broke the rules?

A nightmare he'd be mad to repeat.

'Would you like a proper tour of the main chalet?' he asked. 'Now's the best time, the lull before the storm. Unless Sophie's already shown you?'

'We didn't have time.' Holly bit her lip, a tiny gesture that sent a volt of sexual energy coursing through his veins.

'Okay, follow me.' Scott strode off quickly before the close confines of the hallway led him to do something he shouldn't.

In the main open plan living area mellow flames still flickered in the fireplace. They cast a soft, amber haze over the room's leather sofas and faux fur throws.

'Sheepskin, cow skin… Any other animals to declare?' Holly grinned.

He liked that she was taking the mickey.

'Actually I think the rug under that table over there is goatskin. I know, it's a bit of a cliché but it's what the guests expect. Chalet chic. Looks simple and rustic but costs the earth.'

'I think it's fab. And so lovely to have a real fire too.' She walked towards the hearth, stretching out her hands.

He imagined Holly lying on the rug in front of the fire, her curves highlighted by the soft light.

Clearing his throat, he wrenched his eyes away. 'Do you need to make your phone call or can it wait?'

'It can wait.'

'Follow me.' He led her to the guest suites, striding ahead to make sure she didn't come too close. He wasn't sure how long his resolve might hold. The client accommodation reminded him of his earlier suspicion. He turned to face her.

'You still haven't answered my question. If it wasn't yours, where did the bra come from?'

He couldn't help himself. The question slipped out before he could stop it.

Like steak and chips when you were on a diet, teasing Holly was just too tempting.

'Chalet Repos' lost property.' Her confident stare radiated defiance.

'So our guests pay for the luxury experience and you choose to drape their underwear in public for the whole of Verbier to see?'

'But it's okay to let your staff face some initiation where they have to flash their underwear to the entire resort? I'm quite sure it contravenes some employment law or other.'

Checkmate.

'Why do you want this job?' Genuine curiosity prompted the question.

'Why spend the winter temping in a London office and cram-ming yourself onto the tube when you can ski all day and hit the town at night?'

He'd heard this argument many times. Gut instinct said she

14

was parroting what she'd heard someone else say. Holly wasn't a party animal. Was she going to give him a straight answer to any question he asked?

'Right.' He remained unconvinced. 'Well, it's part of your job to make sure our guests have their every whim met. Whatever the guest wants, from fireworks to an off-piste expedition, we organise it. That's what we do; help them experience life to the max.'

Great, now he sounded like a cola commercial.

'Err, when you say every whim…'

'Every whim within reason that is,' he replied, trying very hard to suppress all the whims he'd like Holly to satisfy. 'Nothing dodgy obviously. Don't worry. Come to me if you have any problems with... ahem, sexual harassment.'

'Like people asking me questions about my underwear for example?' She smiled sweetly.

This girl was trouble.

He grinned. 'Yes… something like that. Right, I'd better dash and let you make that phone call. I've got a date with some paperwork. And another thing – do you mind if I leave your ski pass 'til the morning? I expect you can't wait to hit the slopes.'

'Err, no that will be fine. Well, um, goodnight.' Her eyes searched his for a few seconds before she averted her gaze. Was she looking for something? Hoping for something?

'Goodnight.' He turned away. Walking to his office was one of the strongest tests of self-control he'd ever known.

**

Holly paced the room clasping her iPhone. As it was more of a broom cupboard with bunk beds than a real bedroom this was difficult. She thought about the banter with Scott and smiled. She'd won that last point nicely. Although, what if he now thought she didn't want him to flirt?

Well then, that would be good because she didn't want him to. Did she?

She stared out of the window. The snow fell in thick, heavy flakes as large as her palm. The view of the valley with its snow-laden pine trees and picturesque chalets bathed in the moonlight soothed her.

She scrolled through her contacts list, maybe it was a bit late to ring. She'd text Pippa instead.

Hi Pips. Am in Verbier now at Chalet. Was forced to strip in bar tonight. All your frickin' fault! Can't believe you got me into this!!! Hope things are okay hun xx

A beep signalled a reply.

Hey! Fast work there grasshopper ;-) Landed a zillionaire yet? xx

Hmm, I met a rather interesting guy who kept going on about my underwear... Well, maybe she wouldn't send that reply. Instead she typed:

Get real – I've got to be up at stupid o'clock to clean toilets, no time for zillionaires! Snow is lush though. Wish you were here H xx

Pippa's reply appeared on her screen as she watched.

Put your big girl pants on and go get yourself a man ;-) P xx

Great, why did Pippa insist on assuming all Holly needed was a man? It did Holly's head in. She'd told her often enough she wasn't bothered. What she needed was to be as far away from home as possible and to be left alone. She looked around at the four bunks squeezed tightly into the cramped space.

Alone was something she was going to struggle to be.

'Give us a snog love.' One of the guests leered towards Holly, red-faced and with a paunch that bulged over his waistband, shirt buttons straining.

She reeled back from the alcohol fumes on his breath, almost gagging. The chimes of the church clock rang out the New Year, sounding sharp and clear on the alpine air.

Holly cursed the enforced jollity of New Year and drunken morons... sorry, 'paying guests', to whom she had to be polite and not knee in a sensitive area, no matter how provoked she was.

She'd slip away for a bit. The others could cover for her. If they took cigarette breaks then why shouldn't she have a little nervous breakdown break? She raced down the steps.

The path to Chalet Repos' terrace lay shrouded in darkness, illuminated only by flashes of fireworks. Most of the guests were up on the balcony or inside. The firework display would keep everyone busy for a while.

She inhaled the fresh air deeply, enjoying the relative peace so much that she didn't care about the cold. You'd think a ski resort in the Swiss Alps would have plenty of peace but no such luck. The small dormitory had proved as suffocating as she'd feared.

'Who or what are you escaping from?' A low male voice asked from the shadows.

She jumped up from her slouched position next to a pile of crates, muscles tensed. If anyone tried it on she was using her self-defence moves, guest or no guest.

'Hey, it's okay, don't panic,' he added, the kindness in the tone sounding familiar. Her fists unclenched and she peered at the man more closely, her eyes becoming accustomed to the dim light and recognising Scott.

His eyes gleamed in the darkness, appraising her with an intensity that made her shiver. Frying pans and fires came to mind.

'Hello again.' His mouth widened into a warm, confident smile.

'Hello,' she replied shyly, hoping the darkness partially obscured her thousand-watt smile reaction to seeing him again.

Avoiding tackling her confused emotions for him had been fairly easy since her first night, as he'd flown home to London for Christmas. She'd been up to her armpits with guests' children needing babysitting while their parents skied. Not that she minded being busy but her ski pass lay untouched in her rucksack and she never got round to organising a lesson.

'What brings you down here?'

'I don't want to be kissed.' She blurted the words before her internal censor had time to react.

His handsome face creased with amusement. 'I wasn't planning on kissing you, but now you mention it...'

She could feel her face flaming, even in the freezing night air. Snowflakes stung on her overheated skin. She hated Scott's knack of making her blush like a teenager.

'Come into my office, it's more comfortable than out here. Warmer too.'

'Come into my parlour' said the spider to the fly...

He took her hand, tugging her through the back door and she ignored her reservations, too intrigued to pull back. He exuded a no nonsense air of authority that was hard to resist and seemed infinitely more grown up than the lairy city boys staying at the chalet for New Year. Sure, he was older than them by a few years, maybe about thirty or late twenties, but she didn't think it was just age that set him apart.

'I meant I don't want to be kissed by one of the guests, they've had a bit too much to drink.' It was a huge understatement. They'd been downing champagne at a staggering rate.

She stood awkwardly in his office, aware of her hand still resting in his, skin on skin. The odd sensation they were the only two sober people in the world at that moment made her skin prickle with anticipation.

'But you would like to be kissed by me?' He stroked the palm of her hand with his thumb, a tiny movement but one that set her senses on fire.

Up close the manliness of him overwhelmed her. The attraction drawing her to Scott was so visceral it scared her. He was fit and rugged. His thick, dark hair flopped wherever it pleased and a hint of stubble shadowing his strong jawline. She imagined how that stubble would feel if he kissed her.

'I...'

Kiss me. Please kiss me!

It was no good. She couldn't say the words aloud. But the hot rush of desire was there nevertheless. She tried to remind herself she wasn't here in Verbier for this. The terrifying sense he could see right through her to the Holly hardly anyone knew unnerved her. Fear fought attraction and she felt like the Pushmi-pullyu from Dr Doolittle, not knowing which way she wanted to run.

'Did you have a good Christmas?' She tried to steer the conversation into safer waters.

He shrugged, eyes briefly clouded and his features taking on a harder edge. 'You know families.'

Indeed she did.

'No murders then?' She smiled, hoping to lighten the atmosphere.

'Not yet, I managed to restrain myself.' The corner of his mouth twitched.

'Hey, why do you think I came here for Christmas?' she joked and then instantly regretted it. Kissing would be preferable to questions.

Infinitely more preferable. Was it too late to press the rewind button?

'Running away from guests wanting to kiss you was the better option?'

Actually it was.

'I'm not one of *those* chalet girls,' she murmured, shifting uncomfortably and avoiding his quizzical stare. 'You know, you must know what everyone gets up to?'

'Unofficially yes, officially no.' He regarded her with amused interest. 'As long as everyone involved is over eighteen I don't see I've any business stopping it if two people want to sleep together.'

Sleep together.

The phrase stuck in Holly's mind and her cheeks burned again. Great, how did this guy have the ability to make her blush so easily? She hadn't been like this since her first crush at sixteen.

'So, what sort of chalet girl are you?' He quirked a thick, dark eyebrow. Knowing amusement danced in his eyes and his thumb rhythmically stroked the inside of her palm. The movement started a gentle tingling that spread all over her body.

She had to say something, needed to make it clear bed hopping wasn't her thing. The only one-night-stand she'd had, against her better judgement, left her feeling miserable, not liberated.

'I know it's not fashionable to admit it but I'm not interested in sleeping around.' She tried to tug her hand away but he wouldn't let go.

A steady humming of arousal tickled her skin, spreading up from the rhythmic circles Scott was tracing on her palm.

'That's okay Holly, I don't want you to sleep around. I just want you to sleep with me.'

''Are you teasing me?' she asked.

'Oh, you'll know when I'm teasing you.' He grinned.

She sensed he knew sex, knew it very well and knew how to make it good for her. Suddenly she wanted very much to be teased by him. Heck it was tempting but at the same time bloody scary too.

Turned on beyond the point of no return she couldn't pull away.

'I just want to sit away from the kiss danger zone up there. At least until after everyone's done that midnight, New Year kissing thing. I want to avoid leery, beery idiots and get to bed. Alone that is.' She tried to look like she believed it, as though he wasn't turning her on by what he was doing to her hand.

As though they didn't both know where this was going.

20

Fancying Scott gave him power over her. She knew it and so did he, the knowledge gleamed in his eyes with a triumph that should have annoyed her but excited her instead.

She felt jittery, out of her depth and not knowing how to get back to the shallows. She was definitely in shark territory.

'Leery, beery idiots?' He laughed. 'Would those be the same ones who are paying your wages? So, if you're not one of *those* girls why don't you tell me who you are? You're a bit of an enigma to me.'

'Why? There's nothing to know.' She tugged her hand away. He didn't let go. She could insist. Perhaps she should insist, she knew instinctively if she did then he'd release his grip immediately.

But I don't want him to let go...

Sod it! She didn't know what she wanted.

I want him.

The deep unbidden response roared in her ears.

'I doubt there's nothing to know, Holly.' His eyes gleamed with curiosity. 'So you're here to avoid your family, amongst other things?'

'Why ask if you already know?'

'It's called making conversation, you should try it sometime. But you've avoided my question. I find that interesting.' His eyes searched hers and stripped her bare, body and soul.

Squirming, she hoped he couldn't really see her secrets, her inadequacies and fears. Hoped he couldn't see how different she was from the rest of the seasonnaire crowd. After two weeks in Verbier she still hadn't blended in. His gaze assessed her with the intensity of x-ray vision. He probably knew the colour of her knickers and her bra size by now.

Oh no, her mistake, he'd already worked that out. Some talent. Was that really the kind of guy she wanted to be with?

Yes, yes, yes!

Her body screamed at her to listen. Here was a drop dead gorgeous guy flirting like mad with her and she was resisting... why exactly?

'It's hardly interesting. I'm here to improve my French and to spend time abroad.'

'But not to party? You must be the only one of my employees not drinking tonight.'

'Well, someone has to be sensible, to stay in control.' Her jaw clenched, she resented the implication she was boring. 'You must know what I mean, given you run your own business. You're pretty sober yourself. I haven't seen you drinking so I assume you know exactly what I mean.'

The fact Scott wasn't drinking was a huge plus point in his favour as far as she was concerned.

'Losing control can be fun sometimes Holly.' His thumb circled her palm with increased pressure, his eyes promised far more.

She looked away, confused and half longing for invisibility, half revelling in the knowledge that he saw her, really saw her. She couldn't decide which girl to be. It was easy to fade into the background surrounded by three chalet girls who were attention seeking Divas.

Here with Scott there was nowhere to hide. She was teetering on the edge of something, waiting to see if he would push her.

Waiting to see if she had it in her to jump.

'I, I wouldn't know... I'm still not sure,' she stammered, cheeks hot, feeling sixteen again. The Madonna lyrics played on an internal loop – 'like a virgin, touched for the very first time...'

She'd explode if he didn't kiss her, didn't touch her..

'Wouldn't you like me to show you how losing control can be fun?' His voice was smooth and tempting, like melting caramel. 'I get the feeling you need to be in control. But don't you find it exhausting? Don't you ever long for someone else to take control for you once in a while? I promise you, it'll be fun.'

Her eyes widened, shocked at having one of her deepest desires exposed. How could he know she'd loathed always having to be the adult in the household? That she longed with an intense hunger for someone to come and look after her sometimes, like her friends' mothers did.

She'd felt like she had her nose pressed up against the glass window of a cake shop when she went round to their houses for tea. Not that it happened much because she could never invite them back.

Scott progressed up from the palm of her hand to stroke the pulse point on the tender inside of her wrist. Her heart raced, it was as though he'd stripped her defences away with those few sentences. Her lips parted instinctively and a persistent desire throbbed between her legs.

She edged closer to him, her body giving him the response her lips didn't seem able to. Leaning back, he reached out an arm to lock the door leading into the main chalet then pulled her back with him to a large leather armchair in the corner of the room.

'Will you let me to take control Holly?' he whispered huskily into her ear, the warm breath making the small hairs on her neck prickle with anticipation. 'I'll only ask once. Let go for just ten minutes and I promise when you walk out of here you can take the control right back again.'

Holly's head seemed to nod of its own volition, her body one step ahead of her mind. She sat sideways on his lap, overwhelmed by a mix of emotions she could barely begin to untangle. There was one emotion she couldn't ignore. She wanted him, and it opened a chasm of longing up inside her.

She could feel his erection beneath her thighs and was flattered. Scott was gorgeous and there were lots of hot girls in Verbier who'd kill to be where she was sitting right now. She'd heard enough stories over the past few weeks to know he was making an exception for her. Just thinking about that turned her on even more.

Her head span, being desired was a pretty potent cocktail. It was oh so tempting to let go, to relax for just a few minutes.

When was the last time I really enjoyed myself? Or felt truly relaxed?

She didn't know if the hyper-vigilance had ever truly left her.

'Would you like me to kiss you Holly?' His question cut through her thoughts. It was time for her mind to catch up with her body.

'Yes, I'd like you to kiss me. But I can't have, well, I can't have you know, sex with you not here, not now…' she mumbled, mortified, wishing a trap door would open to swallow her up.

'That's cool. The door's locked. No one will come in. Let me help you relax.'

His touch ripped through her last shred of restraint.

'Okay.' She nodded, her breath catching at the top of her chest as his hand found the hem of her skirt, slid underneath and trailed up her thigh. He traced the edge of her hold ups, tickling and stroking. She gasped as he tickled the bare sensitive flesh at the top of her thigh before caressing the silk fabric of her knickers in a way that made all the breath leave her body.

This should feel too fast, I ought to be protesting… But this is soooo good!

He had her in thrall, wondering what he'd do next, willing to do pretty much anything he asked.

While he stroked the strip of fabric between her legs his mouth found hers and a firm tongue slid between her lips, boldly exploring. Her tongue met his, tasting him hungrily and rough stubble grazed her cheek. The friction of rough against smooth sent a delicious dart of pleasure through her body. Her legs edged further apart, silently begging Scott to touch her.

Please go under the silk. Strip me, touch me, and make me come…

She squirmed and pressed herself against his hand, wanting him but not bold enough to say what she really wanted. Tentatively she reached across to his jeans to caress him but he pushed her hand away.

'No, not now,' he murmured. 'Just relax, Holly. Lie back.'

She obeyed him. Lying back across his lap, she let him push her skirt up around her hips, allowed him to part her thighs with his fingers.

More aroused than she'd ever been before, she squirmed and sighed. He tugged at the buttons of her white shirt and stroked her breasts through their pale pink lacy cups, making her nipples stiffen against the palms of his hands.

'Pink and lacy. I was right.' He announced triumphantly before lowering his mouth to her breasts.

She forgave him for being smug as he kissed and gently nipped her nipples through the lacy bra. Was this what he meant when he'd said he would kiss her? She moaned, wriggling and squirming on his lap, parting her legs a little wider, wanting him to go lower. Needing him to touch her.

'You're beautiful,' he whispered and as though he'd read her mind he stroked a hand down to her stomach, reaching her knickers. He traced rhythmic circles on the surface of the fabric until she was so wet for him she couldn't bear it any more.

'Please,' she groaned, arching up under his hand. He laughed.

'Sure.' He slid two fingers under the elastic and plunged them inside her, thrusting as he kissed her again. Pressure built up between her legs and she writhed against his fingers, wanting more.

'Hang on…' He pulled away from her, his breathing ragged and his eyes dark with lust. Standing up he pushed her back onto the buttery-soft leather and deftly positioning her close to the edge of the chair. Tension vibrated on the air as she waited, still reeling from his caresses.

The only sound in the room was their breathing, Scott exhaling loudly as he slid her knickers down and slipped them into his pocket. She felt achingly exposed, the sensation of air between her legs unfamiliar.

The bulge in his jeans told her he was as turned on as she was. How contrary of her to long for him to make love to her. Yet at the same time she'd be disappointed if he didn't respect her request.

'Don't worry.' Scott crouched down in front of her. 'I asked if I could kiss you and that's all I'm going to do.'

Spooky. He must be able to read my mind. But…

'I didn't say *where* I was going to kiss you though.' He grinned, eyes gleaming.

She couldn't breath, couldn't think as he raised her thighs onto his shoulders. Relief she'd showered earlier mixed with anxiety.

Just what was Scott going to do? 'Oh, my... God.' She moaned softly as his tongue lapped her.

She forgot to be self-concious, forgot to worry how she compared to other girls and pretty soon she forgot to think at all...

He gently circled the most sensitive nub of flesh with the tip of his tongue. She bucked against him, half scandalised, half wild with exhilaration. His hands slid under her bare buttocks, clasping and squeezing them.

She felt like a different creature entirely from the woman who'd walked into the office ten minutes ago. But then Scott's ministrations were a whole universe apart from Paul's lengthy and fumbling attempts to make her come. There was nothing fumbling about what Scott was doing to her right now.

Soon her whole body was overwhelmed by a wave of molten pleasure that practically ripped her out of his hands.

Oh... My... God...

So this was what everyone had been going on about. Well it was pretty damn... amazing. Holly knew that however long she lived, she'd never have a New Year's Eve kiss to beat that one.

She shuddered, quivering as he lowered her carefully back onto the chair.

'Happy New Year, Holly,' Scott said, grinning at her as he pulled her skirt back down.

For a moment his dark eyes stared at her intently, as if to check she was okay.

Then he turned abruptly, unlocked the door and walked back into the chalet corridor as if nothing had happened.

Well... That was...

She bit her lip. Should she wait for him to come back? Or go back up and try to be nice to the guests, make sure they were having a good time. Like she was being paid to.

Shell-shocked, she did up her shirt buttons and rose to go out the back way, needing the fresh air to bring her back to reality.

The sudden rush of cold air between her legs reminded her he still had her knickers.

She felt brazen, liberated and confused all at once. Her legs were a little shaky as she made her way back round to the side entrance.

It was a clear night. The stars shone brightly in the inky blackness with no light pollution to obscure them. She was miles away from London, that was for sure, and a long way from home in more ways than one. She didn't know if what she'd just done, what she'd let Scott do, was fantastic or the worst mistake of her life.

Although her initial desire had been sated she still ached for him, felt incomplete somehow. She needed more.

And she needed her knickers back.

CHAPTER THREE

Scott made his way down the corridor to the kitchen in search of a glass of something cold. An ice cold shower was what he really needed to take the edge off his desire to finish what he'd started with Holly.

A cold shower or a stiff whiskey.

Not that whiskey was an option. He'd trained his body to manage without it. Grief may have tempted him once, the alcohol blurring the sharp edges of the pain of bereavement. But inevitably it had been a false friend and he'd never choose its company again.

Work distraction would have to do instead. It always helped. Pouring every waking moment into expanding Luxury Chalet Experiences rather than torturing himself with guilt paid great dividends. Expanding into Italy to capitalise on the weak euro, while keeping the income in British pounds, was a risky move but one he thought would pay off.

That the business kept him away from London was a happy coincidence. If he had to stay within a ten-mile radius of his family he'd be stark raving bonkers by now.

The murmur of voices reached him from the living room. He ought to go and chat to the guests about the off-piste skiing trip they'd requested, but not yet. Tension wound itself around his

28

body like a tightly coiled spring. He could've done with the release of sex with Holly tonight. It'd been bloody hard walking away.

He headed straight for the fridge as quietly as possible, buying himself a little more time alone. Christmas at home had been hellish as news of his father's most recent infidelity had leaked out. The dishonesty of it riled him. Why couldn't people just be straight with each other? Hadn't they had enough of that in their family already? It had taken his sister Zoë from them and you'd have thought they might learn something from that.

He grabbed a bottle of cold water, trying not to mull on the fact it was almost a year since they'd lost Zoë to cancer. If she hadn't lied about feeling ill they might have got her help sooner, despite her terror of chemo.

Lying should be a capital offence.

He slugged down the water, trying to swallow down his anger with it. A conversation at the other end of the kitchen broke into his thoughts and he tuned in to listen, turning his gaze on Sophie, Magda and Amelia. They had clustered around the kitchen island drinking rather than circulating with guests as they were supposed to. He heard Holly's name and decided to postpone the kick up the behind they needed. After all Holly hadn't been working either...

'Where on earth can she have got to?' Amelia searched for discarded champagne bottles containing dregs and poured the contents into her glass. 'It's not like Miss Goody Two Shoes to play hooky.'

'Perhaps she's shagging someone in the Jacuzzi?' Magda sneered. Drink always made her tongue harsh and her eyes as sharp as flint. It wasn't a look he found attractive, even though her ice-cool Scandinavian looks were the type most men went for.

'Naahhh,' Amelia rolled her eyes. 'Holly wouldn't shag Daniel Craig if he begged her, she's far too uptight. She should neck a few drinks and chill out more.'

'Come on, she's all right.' Sophie grabbed a discarded champagne glass and glugged the contents down.

Scott warmed to her. Sophie was nice, definitely kinder than the other two. He felt glad Holly had someone on her side. Make that two people on her side. The flash of vulnerability on Holly's face when he'd asked about her family roused his protective instincts.

Holly entered the room looking flushed, cute and very, very fuckable. Scott groaned inwardly as the invisible coil tightened its grip on him. Then he moved closer and cleared his throat so the girls were aware of his presence. Their guilty expressions at seeing both him and Holly were quickly replaced as they recovered themselves and plastered smiles on their faces.

'Happy New Year, girls. Enjoying yourselves?' he raised an eyebrow.

'We were just clearing up, Scott,' Magda beamed at him, the queen of bullshit.

'You can clear up in the morning. Go mingle. You need to make sure none of our guests ends up in a snowdrift tonight. Hypothermia might put a bit of a dampener on their holiday.'

Holly smiled and hesitantly met his eye but looked away again quickly when he winked at her.

Irresistible. Concentrate Scott, work!

'Wait a sec girls, while I remember – the day after tomorrow we're taking the guests on an off-piste skiing expedition. We need to be at the helipad by eight am and I want the two best skiers, Magda and Holly to come with us.'

Holly choked on her orange juice and Magda slapped her on the back with what seemed like unnecessary force to Scott.

'Are you okay?' He moved closer, concerned.

'I'm um, fine,' she gasped, stepping out of Magda's reach. 'But I'm really not a very good skier. I don't know why you'd think I was.'

Scott smiled. 'Now I know you're being modest. When you listed skiing as an interest on your CV I'd no idea how many amateur competitions you'd won. The guests will be really impressed to have a slalom champion along side them.'

The colour drained from Holly's face. She looked imploringly at him, aghast. 'Really, I'm not any good, I...'

'Enough with the false modesty Holly,' Amelia snapped, clearly put out to be ousted from the helicopter trip by the new girl. 'If you don't want people to know you shouldn't splash it all over your Facebook page, should you?'

Time to break things up.

'Come on girls, don't get catty on me. Go forth and mingle and don't forget to be professional. Our guests are paying good money to have a nice time and that money pays your salaries so please go do your jobs.'

***

Holly scuttled out of the room before anyone could talk to her but headed for her room instead of the party. She'd left her iPhone on charge and needed to find out what on earth everyone was talking about.

Don't panic, there'll be a rational explanation. You can find this other Holly Buchanan's profile and go show Scott, explain you can't ski.

She grabbed her phone from its charger and clicked immediately onto her Facebook App.

'This can't be right,' she murmured aloud. 'Oh bloody hell!'

On her Facebook Timeline there was a photo of her on skis, holding up a cup... Dazedly she backed onto her bunk bed and sat down. How could this be happening? It all looked so real, for a microsecond she even questioned if she'd some kind of selective amnesia and had simply forgotten she was an expert championship skier.

Get with it Holly, think...

Obviously someone had hacked her account. She clicked on the twitter app too, just to check and gasped as she read 'her' latest tweet.

Gr8 to be back in Alps again, can't wait to show Verbier my moves on the slopes!

She ground her teeth. There it was again, that picture of her on skis, holding a cup. How? Someone must have photo-shopped it. But who… who would do that? Who on earth would think this was funny?

Steve? The answer popped into her mind. He was a techno freak computer nerd and had a pretty warped sense of humour.

She pressed 'Pips mobile' on her contact list, nervously biting at some loose skin on her thumb. Given it was New Year they would still be up, she was sure. After two rings Pippa answered, Holly cut across her greeting.

'Hi there, I need to keep this short because the call's going to cost a fortune.'

'Well, Happy New Year to you to!' Pippa replied.

'Sorry Pips, I'm a bit stressed. Someone's hacked my Facebook and Twitter accounts and posted some rubbish about me being a championship slalom skier. They've even posted a photoshopped photo. Worse still, my boss has seen it and wants me to help take the guests off piste the day after tomorrow.'

'Really? How funny!'

'It is not bloody funny, it's a nightmare,' Holly groaned. 'I put skiing as an interest on my CV, meaning I was interested in learning how to ski and now with that and the Facebook thing he seems convinced I'm an ace.'

'So, tell him the truth.'

'I tried and he just thinks I'm being modest. I didn't actually admit I'd never been on skis before though. Are you laughing?' Holly rubbed at her aching temples with her free hand. What on earth was she going to do?

'Can't you just fudge it, haven't you had any lessons yet?'

'No, I had no time last week. You remember, I had all that babysitting work, looking after the tots while their parents skied.

I hired some skis and boots when I got here and I've got those Salopettes and the ski jacket I managed to get cheap on eBay. But… I think there's a shedload more to it than just having the right gear.' Holly sighed, she just couldn't face admitting she'd never skied, it was too lame.

'Go and talk to him tomorrow. It'll be fine, stop stressing.' Pippa yawned. 'Or you could learn tomorrow, have some kind of crash course in the basics.'

Was that even possible? Holly briefly considered the option, mad as she knew it probably was.

'I'm not sure about that. But Pips, hang on. One other thing I need to ask you – do you have any idea who the hacker might be? I was wondering if, you know, Steve might have done it as a joke.'

'You think Steve did it?' Pippa's tone was sharp now.

'I don't know, it was just a possibility,' Holly backtracked, feeling guilty. 'Sorry, look, give my love to Steve and the bump and if you can think of anyone who might have done this can you let me know?'

'Okay, I will. Now take care and stop stressing. 'Night.'

''Night,' Holly replied and pressed the red button to end the call.

Great, so where did that leave her? She would just have to find Scott and tell him, explain her accounts had been hacked. Sure, she'd put skiing on her CV as one of her hobbies but everyone lied a *little* bit on those kinds of things. He wouldn't mind, surely.

Thinking of Scott reignited the spark of desire still smouldering since his 'kiss' earlier. Would she get a repeat performance? She hoped so. She still ached for him, needed him inside her. Why oh why had she told him she didn't want sex yet?

When she went back up to the party he was nowhere to be found. Relief mixed with anxiety at the postponement. Now it would be hanging over her head all night. Great.

She'd tell him tomorrow, he'd be fine about it. Of course he would.

The skis carried her effortlessly over the glittering snow and Holly grinned across at Scott who skied next to her. He smiled back at her, a sexy smile that promised very exciting things.

When she turned back to the snowy horizon she could see dark obstacles lying ahead in the snow. She looked down at the ground to see her skis had vanished and old tin trays were strapped to her feet instead.

Damn. It was a dream. Of course she was dreaming, after all she couldn't actually ski. She wobbled, her balance faltering. Scott had disappeared up ahead before she could call to him and she tumbled over onto the hard impacted snow, banging her head with a force that left her reeling.

Holly sat bolt upright, chest tight and breaths coming in great gulps. A killer headache thumped away in her head, accompanied by a powerful emotion, a familiar sense of not being good enough.

It was just a dream. It didn't mean anything… She looked at the time – it was only four am. She played Angry Birds on her phone to keep her mind from racing, only falling asleep again just ten minutes before her alarm went off.

***

When Scott failed to appear at breakfast she decided to find him in his office. Her heart thumped painfully hard, sleep deprivation exacerbating her anxiety. There was no answer to her knock so she pushed the door tentatively.

The office was empty.

She stared at the chestnut brown leather armchair in the corner.

Did last night really happen?

Heat rose in her cheeks as flashback images came to mind. Had she really done *that*? With a man she barely knew. Worse than that, with a man who was her boss!

Sensing someone behind her, she turned to find Magda staring at her, a malevolent gleam in her eye.

'Oh, Hi Magda, I was just looking for…'

Magda cut across her. 'He's driven to Cortina again, something to do with his latest venture.'

She pressed her lip-glossed mouth into a smug smile, as if to infer she was party to Scott's personal confidences. The very thought made Holly feel sick. Were Scott and Magda an item? Or had they been? No, she couldn't think about it.

She managed a weak smile. 'Oh, on New Year's Day?'

'He's very passionate about his work, it means more to him than *anything* else.' Magda's eyes raked over Holly, sneering at her super-market jeans and hoodie. Clearly Holly's off duty clothes didn't pass muster. 'Scott and I go back a long way. If there's anything you need to know you should ask me rather than bothering him, he's always terribly busy.'

Miaow. Message received loud and clear.

Magda was the last person she'd go to with any problems. Holly ignored the sharp stirrings of jealousy, remembering instead Scott's interest in her, his eyes on her body, full of desire…

'Looking forward to tomorrow?' Magda asked, her pencilled eyebrows arching skyward.

Holly eyed her with suspicion. Magda always seemed to have so many agendas going on at any given time it was hard to keep track.

'Hmm, well, I might not be going.' She crossed her arms over her chest, wondering how quickly she could extricate herself from this conversation.

'But you've got to,' Magda replied, a flinty look in her eyes. 'Amelia and Sophie have the day off and they've arranged to go to Geneva shopping. They've even booked their train tickets. You can't wimp out now.'

'No problem,' Holly lied. 'I expect it's not that difficult really?'

'It's a really easy run, you could do it in your sleep.' Magda smirked and rolled her eyes as she walked away.

I did do it in my sleep last night and I came a cropper!

Holly chewed thoughtfully at a loose fingernail, hugging her arms around her chest. Sophie, she'd go and find Sophie. Maybe she knew someone, one of the ski instructors who'd give her some cheap intense tuition. After all she had most of today free before she had to be back for supper duty. There was one advantage to the all male group - at least she didn't have to add babysitting to her duties.

Why hadn't Scott told her he was going to Italy again today? After all he'd told Magda...

Come on Holly, it's not like he's your boyfriend or anything. He didn't promise anything and that's... fine.

Yeah right, and if she believed that then she was a championship skier. Once she'd sorted this out she swore she would never lie on her CV again. But then skiing with the guests certainly hadn't been mentioned at the interview.

Scott would be fine about this, surely. Maybe he'd even find it funny?

***

When her alarm went off at six am the next morning she was waiting for it, had been lying awake for ages, stiff with fear. Not to mention stiff and sore from yesterday's intensive skiing lesson. A lesson that made it clear to her just how difficult it would be to complete today's trip and remain in one piece, never mind actually convince anyone she had a clue what she was doing.

It was time to find Scott and confess.

CHAPTER FOUR

Scott arrived in the kitchen just after six am with a black cloud hovering overhead. He needed a cup of coffee. The black mood had haunted him since New Year's Eve. He'd driven down to Sion and walked around the town to distract himself from how much he wanted Holly. Being in close proximity to her at the Chalet had been too difficult to handle.

Never had doing the right thing felt so crap.

It'd gone downhill from there when he'd visited the chalet in Cortina on New Year's Day to find the first fix not completed as planned since his last visit in December. And construction site had been left unsecured. Couldn't he trust anyone to get things right? Clearly the site manager had been lying when he'd assured him all was going well. He ground his teeth just thinking about it.

Adding to that was the difficulty of not dwelling on today's date. Zoë died a year ago today and he couldn't bear to think about it. Yet not thinking about her felt like a betrayal.

If she hadn't lied about being ill... If only I'd been around to force her to get medical help...

The old tormenting thoughts pelted him like bullets of hail, stinging as they hit their target.

The only glimmer of sunshine that morning was Holly, looking up from the sink where she dried the saucepans from last night's supper. She was keen, there was no sign of the other girls yet. Her auburn waves were secured up in a loose ponytail and her cheeks flushed a healthy pink.

A real English Rose.

'Morning,' she said, smiling tentatively.

'Hi there, looking forward to today?' He found he was able to smile back at her. His spirits had lifted already at the thought of spending the day with her, and hopefully the night too, if all went as planned.

'That's what I wanted to talk to you about.' She twisted and untwisted the tea towel in her hand.

'Not bailing out on me I hope?' The disappointment was crushing. He'd regretted not asking her to go with him to Cortina yesterday. So what if the other girls had talked? Sod them. He wanted to spend time with Holly and he was the boss. If anyone was allowed to break the rules, he could. 'I'm relying on you to help and it'll be great fun.'

'I'm not that good at skiing you know.' She bit her lip. 'I have no idea where that photo on the Internet came from. It must be someone's idea of a joke.'

He could hardly concentrate on what she was saying. Memories of Zoë's final days in the hospice in Surrey had unleashed a torrent of pain. Awareness of Holly's reluctance to join the trip today penetrated his thoughts but he couldn't listen. He needed her with him, even if that made him selfish. He had to be selfish today if he was going to get through it.

'I'm not expecting too much. Don't worry. Have you got stage fright? It's not that difficult a run, I wouldn't risk real live guests on anything too dangerous.'

'It's... I'm terrified of helicopters,' she blurted. 'Always have been, I'm afraid.'

The tea towel twisted into a tightly knotted rope in her hands, her nails embedded in the cloth.

'Oh? It's a very short ride.' He frowned at her, perplexed. 'You'll barely be strapped in before we land again.'

'I, I don't know.' She squeezed her eyes shut.

'Please do this for me Holly, I don't have time to make other arrangements.' He gazed at her imploringly. 'I'll look after you, I promise. And you know how much the guests like you.'

'Hmm.' She shrugged.

It was true, Holly had been a real hit with the guests. Her softer, caring nature made her more popular than the spiky tongued Magda. He stepped forward and took hold of the tea towel, tugging her towards him and planting a quick, soft kiss on her lips.

Delicious.

Who cared what anyone else thought?

She tasted of coffee and croissants. The sounds of the guests getting up and going to their ensuite bathrooms made him pull back with regret.

'Tonight, after supper, I've got a treat for you.' He squeezed her hand. 'Come on, ski with me today. It's a doddle. Just a gentle run on pristine powder snow. What could be nicer than that? And I promise the helicopter will be fine, over before you know it. Please?'

'Alright then.' She smiled but it was a small, tight smile. 'As long as you know I'm not that good a skier.'

Magda had told him Holly was shy when it came to talking about her achievements. It'd been her who'd shown him Holly's Facebook page. He supposed Holly must be one of those people who had more confidence when in their 'online' persona.

Slalom skiing was highly skilled. Even if she'd lost her nerve for the kind of speeds she was used to in competitions she'd still be streets ahead of the rest of them.

He really wanted her company, the thought of having her by his side lifted his spirits and his day started to look up. If Holly wasn't with him he knew he'd just obsess about Zoë. Holly would be a lovely distraction and the night he'd planned for them would be the perfect ending to the day.

***

Not that good a skier!

The hum of the helicopters rotor blades seemed to resonate with the panic coursing through Holly's body. What on earth had possessed her? She'd hoped pretending to be terrified of helicopters might do the trick.

Clearly not.

It wasn't the helicopter making her nervous but the plunging-head-first-into-an-icy-ravine-when-she-lost-control part. She'd gone for the crash course lesson yesterday on the basis at least she wouldn't have to admit to Scott she'd never skied before in her life. So, she knew how to walk in ski boots, no mean feat in itself, and how to stay upright-ish on skis. She mentally ran through how to execute stopping and turning. As long as she remembered which way she was supposed to lean she might come out of this alive…

Go and tell him you're not doing it!

She ignored the persistent anxiety leaping up and down at the edge of her mind waving a red flag. She hated conflict, absolutely loathed it and would do all kind of stupid things to avoid it. Like this for example. You hardly needed to be a psychologist to know the fear stemmed from her mother's drunken verbal attacks on her but that didn't help her any.

Six hours intensive tuition had left her muscles sore and cramped. Who knew what state she'd be in after today? Nursing broken bones in hospital probably.

Her stomach lurched. Exactly how had she let herself be swept along with this? On the plus side the fact she was clearly lacking a backbone would come in useful later when she hurtled off the edge of the cliff.

She hadn't been able to bear letting him down. He seemed really keen to have her along today and in return she'd wanted to be with him. What surprise did he have planned for her later, she wondered. Would she still be in one piece to enjoy it?

Her fingers knotted together on her lap, knuckles white as she tried to smile at Scott.

'Okay?' he mouthed at her over the noise of the helicopter.

Huh, she wasn't so much okay as certifiably insane. She nodded warily, her stomach lurching in sympathy. She was too far in to tell the truth now. She was sick of always having to pretend she was all right. Just for once she felt like saying 'No, I'm bloody well not okay.'

Magda, sitting next to her, caught her eye and smirked. Almost as if she knew the mess Holly was in. Hmm, maybe it'd been Magda who'd hacked her Facebook and Twitter accounts? She certainly didn't seem to like Holly; she'd taken against her from the first night. But did she really hate her enough to stitch her up like this? Then there was the question of whether she had the technical skills to do it. But even if she didn't, she could easily have persuaded someone who did...

Holly concentrated on taking a deep breath, mentally shelving the suspicion. She needed to concentrate and would just have to do her best. Panicking wasn't going to get her anywhere. She'd have to remember what Finn had taught her yesterday and take it as slow as possible.

All too soon they were landing. Magda climbed out gracefully. Holly lost her footing and slipped on the impacted ice, tumbling face down into the snow.

Even with her face stuck in a snowdrift and stinging with cold, the hoots from the guys descending from the helicopter behind her were audible.

'Here, let me help you up,' Scott said, a strong arm raising her up and setting her on her feet again. 'Right, let's get the gear out the back. I thought Magda and I could take the lead as we know the route to the mountain cantine and you could take the rear, make sure we don't lose a guest on route?'

Humph, losing one of those jerks would be a bonus.

She held her tongue and tried to regain her dignity, last sighted somewhere in a snowdrift. Both her face and her pride smarted like mad, she hated looking stupid. At the rear would be good. No one would be watching her and she could go as slowly as she liked.

Thankfully she managed to get her skis on and locked into position without falling over again or needing Scott's help. The vivid blue expanse of sky contrasted sharply against the jagged, bright-white mountaintops. The air smelt deliciously fresh and mellow sunshine lifted her spirits. Maybe she could enjoy today after all, it couldn't be too…

You have got to be joking? We're going down there?

She eyed the steep mountainside with pure terror, made worse by the sound of the helicopter rotary blades starting up. Once the helicopter left she'd have no choice but to ski down there.

'Scott,' she called out to where he was talking to a guest up ahead, giving him some pointers.

Apparently he hadn't heard. He didn't turn his head and skied off ahead with the guys and Magda. She'd have to ski after them if she wanted to get his attention.

Lean forward, not back, bend your knee to turn… Oh God help me!

Not a regular prayer, she prayed now, not quite sure who she was praying to. *I'll pray to anyone who'll listen!*

She had to catch Scott up before he went too far. She leant forward to increase her speed as she'd been taught. Her stomach lurched and seemed reluctant to keep pace with the rest of her body. She couldn't blame it, the speed terrified her. She seemed to be travelling at a terrific rate and yet she still lagged at the back.

Too late. They'd approached the first ridge.

Please God help me. Don't let me die.

She whispered a prayer as she went over the edge of the pristine powder snow, feeling a disconcerting lurch in her ribcage. Only when she found herself at the bottom of the steep incline and on a gentler slope did she remember to breathe again.

Every muscle tensed, her entire body on high alert. If this run went much further she thought she might literally die of terror. She sped up to keep them in sight, thinking maybe she might just pull this off when her ski hit a ridge in the snow and she lost her balance. She flew into the air and then crashed down onto her back with a force that winded her.

Her back must be broken at the very least. A molten hot pain radiated up through the elbow she'd shot out to try and break her fall.

'Help, help!' she shouted as loudly as she could and tried in vain to push herself up into a sitting position.

The mountain air didn't bring back an answering cry. Winded, exhausted and miserable, she gave up trying to sit up and lay back in the snow. At least her Ebay snow gear was keeping her dry and warm, but for how long? She would just rest a bit and then try again… but what about her phone?

With relief, she remembered her iPhone and pulled it out of her pocket.

No signal.

Of course there wasn't a bloomin' signal. There weren't any mobile phone masts up here on the mountaintops.

They'd find her. Someone would find her. Scott would retrace his steps. Maybe he'd recall the helicopter? She shuddered to think how much it might cost to get her back down. Would her cheapo Internet travel insurance pay out? Probably not, given this was entirely her own fault. Hadn't the winter sports section of the policy said something about off piste skiing? Something like idiots who attempted it deserved all they got, although not quite in those words.

She forced herself to try and sit up again, this time she managed it. Okay, so her back wasn't actually broken after all, but the knock to her elbow had been vicious and the pain was pretty bad. The silence unnerved her as she waited, wondering what she should do.

Then Scott's head and bright red ski jacket appeared over the brow of the slope and she sagged back into the snow with relief. His skis were over his shoulder as he made his way determinedly back to her, his face grim and the snow well up to his knees.

I hope I haven't blown it with him. He looks rather pissed off.

43

She cradled her elbow as it got her attention with another angry stab of pain.

'Holly, are you okay?' he asked as soon as he was in earshot, his eyes full of concern. 'What happened?'

'I'm not sure, I hit something and came over.' She winced as another wave of pain hit her.

'Where are you hurt?' He crouched in front of her.

'My elbow, and my back a bit.' She grimaced again as another wave of pain hit her and cradled her injured arm.

'Let me see your elbow.' His voice was taut with what could have been anxiety or anger, she couldn't tell which.

She shrugged off the ski jacket on the injured side and rolled up the long sleeve of her T-shirt. Even now, in pain and humiliated, his touch on her bare skin roused her libido. Desire fought with embarrassment at being shown up and anger he hadn't listened to her when she'd tried to get out of this trip.

The pain wasn't helping her mood much either.

'I think it might be a ligament injury. We'll have to get you back to town to a doctor.'

'I did try to tell you I wasn't an experienced skier.'

'What?' he frowned, his forehead furrowed. 'But what about all that stuff on your Facebook page? Are you seriously trying to tell me it was faked?'

'It wasn't faked by me,' she said quickly, alarmed by the hard expression that had crept into his eyes, driving the softer Scott deep under cover. 'Someone must have hacked my account, faked the photo on Facebook and well… thought it was a joke.'

He looked at her closely, still frowning. Anger surged through Holly, why couldn't he just take her word for it? What was so hard to understand?

'Hmm. But who on earth would do that?'

'I don't know,' she answered tersely. He didn't believe her, clearly thought she was some kind of nutcase.

She wanted the caring Scott back again, but the connection

between them had clouded over, shutters being pulled down as they spoke. The knowledge of it pierced her with a pain much sharper than the throbbing in her elbow.

Sitting back and letting this happen was not an option. She had to fight her corner.

'It's the truth, I had nothing to do with that post.' She glared at him.

'But you said on your CV you could ski.' The narrowed eyes continued to appraise her, not giving an inch.

'What's this? The Swiss inquisition? I, I listed it under hobbies,' she stuttered indignantly. 'I didn't realise it was going to be part of the job. It wasn't mentioned at interview. I meant I was interested in learning how to… I mean how to improve my skiing.'

'So you have skied before?'

'Yes.' She sighed, realising she had to say more, had to tell him the whole truth. It mattered she was honest, with him of all people. 'But I only had my first lesson yesterday.'

'Yesterday? Bloody hell, when you said you weren't "that good a skier" you actually meant you weren't any kind of skier! You could have been killed up here, how could you have been so stupid?'

Holly gaped at him, the horror on his face seemed out of proportion to what had happened. She regretted telling him the truth now.

Why exactly did I feel the need to be quite so honest with him?

'We'd better get you standing up.' He exhaled and shook his head at her, his tone polite but cool. 'We need to check there are no other injuries.'

She let him help her up, enjoying the sensation of the strong, muscular arms supporting her but seething inwardly that he'd called her stupid. She wanted him to apologise, to fold her into his arms and tell her it didn't matter.

What if this is the last time he ever touches me?

Pain pricked at her eyelids and she blinked it back. She'd invested far too much far too soon. It was her own fault. She shouldn't have let him do… what he did on New Year's Eve.

He held Holly for longer than was necessary for her to get her balance and seemed to hesitate, the rigid set of his jaw softening. 'Are you in pain? The skidoo will be here soon and it can take you straight to the doctor, I'm sure he'll give you something for the pain.'

'We can still do what you had planned this evening, can't we?' She wished she had it in her to play it a bit cooler. Really she was rubbish at this.

She knew why she'd told him the truth. She needed him to know the real Holly, not the chameleon Holly who always tried her best to fit in and not be noticed.

'We'd better see what the doctor says.' His arms remained around her yet there was tension, a combative element to their stance.

She didn't know if she wanted to kiss him or slap him for being so hard on her for a minor offence. Irritation flared within her, what gave him the right to be so judgemental?

'How long will the skidoo be?' she asked.

'Magda was going to fetch one of the guys. They'll be at the mountain café by now so it shouldn't be long.'

'Good old Magda.' She wished she could bite the words back but it was too late.

'Why do you say that?' Scott frowned.

'I think she hacked my accounts. After all she doesn't like me.'

'Come on now, why would she do that? Isn't that a little paranoid?' He sighed. 'To tell the truth I don't know what to think and I could really do without this today of all days.'

His eyes briefly flashed with pain.

"Today of all days".

What did that mean? If she hadn't been so riled she might have stopped to ask.

'Paranoid? Someone set me up!' Holly's jaw clenched and her fighting hackles rose.

'So you've said but Holly, don't you get you could've been killed

46

up here? It's not a run for beginners.' His exasperation was clear but something more than that, he was seriously rattled.

I don't understand what's going on.

'I did try to tell you but you weren't listening,' she said, some of the anger draining away with the realisation he'd been afraid for her. She sighed and rested her head against his chest. His heartbeat pulsed rhythmically in her ear, far more rapid than it should have been.

She didn't know what to say to make this right. The engine of a skidoo broke the silence.

He patted her on the back, almost absentmindedly and disengaged himself, walking in the direction of the noise and waving. 'Over here.'

Before the skidoo reached them he turned back to her. 'You'll be alright with Sven and the doctor will look after you. I'll see you later, back at the chalet.'

Then without another word he snapped his skis back on and was off.

Frickin' brilliant. Well done Holly, you handled that well.

She tried to muster a smile for the tanned and smiling Sven and climbed on board behind him, refusing to lie on the stretcher tied to the skidoo. Things were embarrassing enough without arriving back at the resort on a stretcher with everyone staring at her, hoping to witness a drama.

***

Scott knew he'd behaved badly. Anger at himself, at Holly, and even at Zoë coursed around his body. Confused thoughts whirled in his mind with the intensity of a snowstorm, obscuring any clear thinking as he skied down to catch up with the group.

Perhaps he should've told her about Zoë's anniversary, explained why he'd wanted her with him today and why he was in such a foul mood. But he'd been so furious she'd lied and put herself in danger, just like Zoë had...

He took little pleasure in the breathtakingly gorgeous surroundings. All he could think of was Holly, Holly, Holly.... Lying in his arms, underneath him, her soft curves yielding, her sweet mouth grinning at him and vibrant eyes locking on his. Part of him wanted to go to the doctor with her but he badly needed to get away to calm down, to think...

Had she tried to tell him? He'd been a bit distracted, maybe she'd said something this morning but she certainly hadn't told him she'd never been on a pair of skis in her life! The whole Facebook thing was a weird but perhaps he'd been too quick to judge?

When he stopped to think about it Holly was different from the others, less artificial and certainly not a game player. If he was going to choose between believing Magda or Holly he knew which girl he'd pick, despite Magda having worked for him for two seasons. Maybe he should take her word for it about her accounts being hacked.

He recalled the expression on Holly's face when left her. Guilt twisted inside him. But it wasn't like she was his girlfriend.

No, but you want her to be...

It was true. He wanted Holly more than he could remember wanting anyone. He wanted her to be his, the thought of any of those ski bum instructors getting their hands on her lovely curves wound him up, big time.

He skied on towards the mountain cantine where the group were stopping for lunch.

Give her a chance – you don't meet many Hollys in a lifetime.

The thought popped into his mind, accompanied by a desire so strong it carried him along in its wake, helpless to resist. He'd tell her why complete honesty was so important to him, explain how afraid he'd been when he went back to find her, terrified something terrible had happened, fear gripping at his chest.

He still liked her. Liked her very much indeed.

He thought about what he'd planned for the evening as he parked his skis in the rack and walked round to the front of the café where his group sat sunbathing on the red and white striped café deck-chairs, beers in hands.

'Is Holly okay?' Fake sympathy oozed from Magda's every pore. This was the real picture of insincerity, not Holly.

He could trust Holly.

'She's hurt, but not too badly,' he replied curtly, staring at Magda and wondering if she knew about what had happened between him and Holly on New Year's Eve. He'd have thought Magda would be over what happened last year when he'd rejected her advances. After all she'd applied to come back again this season.

Perhaps Magda wasn't cool about what'd happened. He sighed, Holly's theory made sense. If he hadn't been battling with demons today he might have realised earlier it wasn't that Holly was paranoid but that he was naïve.

He owed her an apology.

CHAPTER FIVE

Holly let herself back into Chalet Repos, exhausted but relieved when she remembered Amelia and Sophie were out for the day. Finally she had a bit of space.

At least the pain in her elbow wasn't so bad now. She grabbed a glass of water and swallowed a couple of ibuprofen before making herself a sandwich in the chalet kitchen.

The doctor had said something about her elbow popping out of the ligament or something like that. Her French hadn't been up to the complex translation. He'd done something hideously painful, charged her the equivalent of her last week's wages for the privilege and now she had the battle of trying to claim it back from her insurance.

She couldn't understand Scott's belligerence. He seemed pretty cool and laid back about most things, which only made his behaviour all the more puzzling. His snap judgement of her still rankled. Yes she'd been stupid but it wasn't like she'd done anything criminal or hurt anyone… well, not yet anyway.

Give me time.

She was certainly tempted – an image of Magda sprang to mind, smug and laughing with Scott over lunch up at the mountain cantine. No doubt she'd be making jokes about Holly, flirting with him and placing perfectly manicured nails on his thigh as she casually reached across the table for the bread…

Holly ground her teeth. Why Magda hated her she didn't know, but her intuition was ringing loud alarm bells. Magda had set her up and she'd walked straight into the trap. She wouldn't find her such an innocent victim next time round, and if Holly found evidence to support her suspicions then she'd no reservations about ringing Steve to see what he could do with Magda's Facebook page…

And if Scott planned to sack her she'd damn well make the most of the chalet today. She hadn't used the Jacuzzi yet, too worried about groping hands and accidental leg brushes under the water from the city boys who were staying this week and too frantically busy last week.

Now was the perfect time to unpack her bikini.

Lying back in the Jacuzzi tub with her eyes closed and the hot water bubbling, easing away tension, she could understand why it was so popular after skiing. The heated water caressed her aching muscles and all her tightly wound worries and stresses slowly dissolved away.

She inhaled the deliciously fresh mountain air and relaxed, feeling more herself again. Sod Scott, she'd find a job somewhere else if necessary. The cafes in the resorts were always looking for English speakers and her French was passable, at least when it came to food and drink.

Soon Holly wasn't thinking of anything at all, just concentrating on the powerful jets as they massaged her thighs, her back and the space between her legs… She couldn't help but think of Scott, of his mouth exploring her most sensitive flesh, caressing her with such surprising tenderness and generosity. Giving her a pleasure more intense than she'd imagined possible.

'Hi.' Scott's real voice broke through her daydream.

She sat up with a start, splashing through the surface of the water.

'Oh, I thought you'd be out for the rest of the day.' She blinked a few times, dazed by the transition from fantasy to reality. 'You don't mind me using the Jacuzzi do you? Only you said it was okay…'

'What? No, of course it's okay. I came back to see if you were all right. The group have turned out to be pretty experienced skiers so I've left Magda to look after them.' He crouched down beside the Jacuzzi.

She tried hard not to stare at his powerful thighs, at the strong hands that had stroked and caressed her so expertly. Tried to remember why she was angry with him...

'I wanted to say sorry,' he added more softly and laid a hand on her shoulder. 'I didn't give you a proper chance to explain. I shouldn't have left you with Sven but taken you to the doctor myself. What's the diagnosis?'

'Some weird ligament thing I think, but the doctor popped it back in. I'm okay really. Look, I'm sorry too, I should have been more insistent when I tried to tell you I wasn't a good skier. I was stupid to think I could fudge it and I'm sorry I gave you a scare,' she replied.

Scott exhaled, his tight jaw relaxing and some of the tension seeming to drain from his face.

Did he want to take up where they'd left off as much as she did? Desire stirred inside her like a lazy snake uncoiling. Her nipples stiffened, visible through her bikini top. The cold air didn't help.

Scott's gaze lowered to her chest, a slow smile creeping across his face. 'You know we have the chalet to ourselves? Magda and the guests won't be back until at least five and Sophie and Amelia are spending the evening in Geneva.'

'Oh, really?' She tried to sound causal and failed miserably.

'So, if you're okay what do you think about getting out of the tub and saying hello properly?'

The sparkle was back in his eye, whatever clouds there had been between them seemingly blown away. The breath left her body.

She'd been pretty much ready for him from the moment he touched her shoulder.

'Okay.' Any last vestige of shyness ebbed away as she stood up, revelling in the feel of his eyes on her body and the dilated pupils betraying his desire.

He wants me. The thought gave her courage and a newfound awareness of her sexual attractiveness. She thought she might do anything he wanted if he had the power to make her feel like this.

He took her hand to help her out of the Jacuzzi and tugged her back towards the chalet. She was happy to let him take the lead. She could trust him.

She did trust him, at a level deeper than conscious thought.

He led her to the living room fireplace. Holly was glad she'd stoked the fire when she got back from the doctors and had put fresh logs on it. The dancing flames licked at the logs in a sensuous way that reminded her of Scott's fingers and tongue exploring her body.

If he didn't do something soon she'd explode.

He tugged at the strings of her bikini top and bottoms and as they fell to the floor he stared at her naked body as though he were appreciating a painting. The heat from the fire warmed her wet skin.

Too impatient to wait, she stepped forward and tilted her head up to kiss him, her hands around his neck and her fingers in his hair, her tongue probing and exploring his mouth, wanting to go deeper and deeper. Wanting, or rather needing to move things on she slid her hands down and up underneath his T-shirt, desperate to feel skin on skin and delighting in the taut, firm flesh she discovered.

Her fingers explored his hard chest and nipples and she provocatively pressed her own bare breasts against his flesh, her nipples twitching and budding even harder against his warm skin.

His erection stiffened, hard as granite against her stomach through his Salapettes. He broke off the kiss, breathing heavily as he yanked his T-shirt off and slid quickly out of his other clothes, seeming in as much of a hurry as she was.

'I want you,' she whispered in his ear, feeling liberated and surer than she'd ever been about a first time. She didn't want there to be any doubt about what she needed. She shivered with anticipation, willing him to hurry up, not wanting anything to come between them again.

'The feeling's mutual. Although I have to say I was looking forward to having to persuade you.'

He reached out and trailed one finger from her collarbone down to her abdomen, stopping tantalisingly above her pubic bone.

'Mmm, that sounds… like fun.' Urgent need throbbed between her legs. 'But I think I need you to speed up to the part where you fuck me.'

He raised both eyebrows, pretending to be shocked. She smiled, backing away to position herself on the rug in front of the fire, glad she had the power to surprise him. She slowly parted her legs for him, training her eyes on his face, watching for the answering gleam in his eyes and enjoying her power to turn him on. After all why shouldn't she take the lead?

'Wait,' he exhaled audibly as he reached for a foil packet from his jacket pocket.

'Would you… like me to do it?' she asked tentatively. He nodded and handed it to her, kneeling in front of her, his eyes as solemn as she'd ever seen them.

This means something to him, I'm sure of it. I'm not just another lay.

I mean something.

She slid it on, sheathing him and growing even wetter with anticipation when she realised how hard he was for her.

'Are you going to finish what you started then?' Her breath caught in her chest. She hadn't breathed properly since the moment he'd spoken, breaking her daydream.

'Am I ever.' His eyes flickered with desire, sweeping appreciatively over her body.

He lay down beside her, kissing her mouth, her neck, her breasts, while all the time stroking her between her legs. She squirmed under his touch, dripping wet for him already and desperate to feel him inside.

Impatiently she angled herself against him.

'Please,' she gulped. 'I need you inside me. Now.'

He rolled over and raised himself on his arms above her, pressing the tip of his erection between her legs, waiting for an agonising moment before he entered her. Then he thrust while she ran her hands over his back and buttocks, pulling the whole length of him deeper inside her, moaning softly as he took her.

Sex had never felt so right, so utterly intoxicating.

'That's... God that feels so good,' she gasped, arching back against him, wriggling on the soft cow-skin rug, enjoying the sensations rippling through her body. Soon she was beyond speech, immersed in a tide of pleasure as endorphins saturated and sated her body.

As the wave of pleasure ebbed, Scott cried out, tensing and shuddered inside her. For a moment he lay on top of her and she didn't mind his weight but clasped him to her. They lay still that way for a while. She liked that he'd come inside her at last. It felt right, necessary to her somehow.

She slowly exhaled and then took her first proper, deep breath since he'd disturbed her in the Jacuzzi.

He rolled off and lay down close beside her. 'I might have to discipline you, you know.'

'Oh, why?' She turned her head on the rug to stare into his eyes, so close their noses were almost touching.

'Sex with other members of staff is forbidden,' he replied solemnly.

'Get stuffed,' she snorted with laughter and then grabbed a faux fur cushion from the sofa, lobbing it at him. He caught it and lobbed it back at her and soon they were having a boisterous pillow fight with the cushions.

Holly laughed until her chest ached. Then she caught a glimpse of herself in the large pine mirror.

Who is that girl? She looks happy.

She collapsed back down on the rug, lying on her back. 'I'm knackered, all this sex and skiing is too much for me.'

'I hope not. I've a surprise planned for tonight.' He rolled on his side and played with her hair, twisting it around his fingers as he spoke.

'Not night skiing. Please not night skiing.' She shuddered theatrically.

'You'll have to wait and see, but right now I have something else I need to do.'

'Oh?' she tried to keep her disappointment from showing.

I'm so crap at playing it cool.

'Yes, I have something I need to finish. I did say it might take some time, and I'm not sure I got it right first time round…' He broke off to kiss her and then he produced a fresh foil packet. 'I want to make love to you again.'

Make love, not sex!

Yes, she was in no doubt this was now about making love. It was a phrase she'd never used before when it came to sex, deeming it too corny, too out of touch with the reality.

But it felt right to describe… this… thing that was happening between them. He cradled her beneath him as he pushed himself deep inside her, holding her gaze, staring into her eyes in a way that made her feel truly connected, truly one with him.

Then slowly, very slowly, he began to rock inside her until the wave of pleasure roared through her body, sweeping away her anxieties and flooding her senses again.

Peace and contentment radiated through her sated body. For the first time she'd met a man she didn't have to pretend to be someone else with, a man who seemed to like the real Holly, preferred her even.

Boy, was that a good feeling.

***

Scott's Landrover barely registered the snow and thick ice on the roads. Holly drank in the winter wonderland scenery, the snow reflecting white in the car's headlights. She loved the tiny lights of the villages, twinkling unbelievably high up in the mountains and admired the floodlit castles of Sion, providing a dramatic backdrop for the valley.

'I'll tell you where we're going when we get there,' Scott replied to Holly for the umpteenth time.

They drove high up into the mountains, eventually taking a concealed turning down to what looked like a new chalet-hotel complex.

'It's a brand new development,' Scott said. 'It's due to open next week but the owner owes me a favour and has given us the exclusive use of it tonight. It's the natural thermal baths and Jacuzzi complex around the back that we're visiting.'

'But I haven't got my swimming costume,' she said, and then flushed as he turned to her and raised an eyebrow.

'It's very private, don't worry.' He grinned. 'Only the mountain Marmots will be able to see what we get up to and I think they've probably got better things to do.'

'You're a very bad man, Mr Hamilton.' Holly attempted a prim voice.

'I know I am. Isn't it fun?'

'I'm reserving judgement.' She turned to look out of the window but was smiling.

For the first time since she'd got to Verbier she hadn't flinched inwardly at the word 'fun'.

In fact, she realised with a start, *I am having fun*.

She felt free, carefree in a way she'd never felt before.

They parked in the deserted car park. Plastic sheeting and scaffolding still adorned part of the chalet building but mellow, low-level lighting lit the surrounding grounds and pool complex.

'It looks magical.'

'I'm glad you like it. Better than night skiing?' He joked.

'Definitely. But are you seriously expecting me to swim outside, naked? Your car temperature gauge read well below freezing on the way down here and look, it's snowing again.'

They both gazed up at the soft, powdery snowflakes now falling steadily, adding to the substantial fall beneath their feet.

'If you've never been swimming in the snow, you haven't lived. The water is really warm, like a giant hot bath. Trust me. Just look at the clouds of steam coming up from the water.' He tugged her towards the entrance and pulled out a set of keys to let them into the indoor complex.

'Well, come on then.' He pulled his jumper and T-shirt over his head. 'Or am I going to have to undress you?'

'Just you try,' she answered and shrieked when he advanced with clear intent in his eyes.

He grabbed her by her hoodie and they ended up in a tangle of limbs on one of the very stylish loungers.

When they stopped laughing, they kissed, hands stroking, exploring and removing clothing, until Holly didn't know where she ended and he began.

'I like you a lot, Holly Buchanan.' Scott stroked the side of her face and held her chin so he could look into her eyes.

'I like you too.' Holly wriggled against him, enjoying the intimacy, basking in that lovely sensation of having all night to make love with Scott. No desperate hurry, just pure, decadent indulgence.

We have all the time in the world.

'Let's swim.' He stood up and she followed him over to the indoor pool that in turn lead outside to the natural thermal pools.

'You're nuts.' She lowered herself into the pool. But the temperature of the water surprised her, the heat enveloping her like a hug. It was as though she'd stepped into a giant's piping hot bathtub. 'Oh, it's lovely.'

'I told you. You really should have more faith in me,' he replied, lifting up the plastic flap that stopped the cold air from entering the building so they could swim underneath it to the outdoor pool complex. In this outdoor pool numerous jets cascaded into the pool and several areas were taken over by bubbling hot Jacuzzi shelves shaped like cradle beds.

'Oh Fab!' Holly swam over to one of the Jacuzzi beds and scrambled up, letting the jets ease away any last vestiges of self-consciousness. 'How do we get to the original natural pools?'

A faint aroma of sulphur hung in the otherwise pure mountain air and steam billowed from the natural pools tumbling from the mountain source. Clearly no amount of snow or sub-zero temperatures could cool them.

'We have to walk over the snow barefoot.' He grinned at her.

'You're joking?' She looked doubtfully at the thick layer of snow that lay between them and the natural pools. 'They do look pretty though, almost magical with all that steam, like dry ice.'

'They are magical,' Scott replied, poker-faced.

'Oh really, so what happens?'

'You have to make a wish.' He kept a straight face, only his lips twitching.

'Let's go then.' She hoisted herself out of the pool and shrieked as her feet sank into the snow. The latent warmth of the Jacuzzi sustained her until she made it to the steaming natural pools.

She sank down into the pool gratefully and Scott jumped in next to her.

'I'm impressed,' he said. 'I thought I'd have to drag you kicking and screaming through the snow.'

'You would have liked that, wouldn't you?' She rolled her eyes. 'I'm sure there's a bit of caveman in you.'

She giggled as he moved closer to her, kissing her neck and running his hands over her breasts beneath the surface of the hot water. He found and gently squeezed her nipples, then cupped them as he increased the intensity of his kisses.

'There's a bit of caveman in every man.' He paused and looked up, directly into her eyes. 'Would you like me to demonstrate?'

'Not yet, I haven't made my wish,' she protested.

'Okay, let's make our wishes. Mine is quite serious though.'

'Oh?'

'Whoever I'm seeing romantically, and right now I'm hoping that will be… well, you Holly. I need that person to be one hundred per cent straight with me. That's all I need.'

'That's your wish?' Holly frowned, was he accusing her of lying or… 'Are you talking about my CV thing again? I thought we were over that?'

'Hey, we are.' He planted a soft kiss on the top of her head. Her hair was covered with snowflakes by now but she still felt deliciously warm. 'I do have an… issue, I suppose you'd call it about people lying to me. I'll tell you why sometime. The thing is, I like you as you are, Holly. You don't need to pretend to be like the other girls. I like it that you're not. It's okay to be yourself, I quite like the real Holly Buchanan, as I was saying earlier.'

His foot gently nudged hers under the water and she knew he meant to reassure her. Frankly she didn't know what to feel. Massive relief that Scott understood her and had given her permission to stop trying to blend in competed with terror she hadn't succeeded, that she'd so obviously stood out.

The real Holly Buchannan suddenly felt naked in more ways than one and it scared her.

'Hey, are you okay?' He nudged her again. 'Why don't you tell me your wish?'

'That I could always feel as free and happy as I feel with you.' The answer tripped off her tongue before she'd even thought about it.

'We'd better make sure we're together a lot then.' He nuzzled her neck and stroked her breasts again.

Soon her misgivings were forgotten. She kissed Scott back with a hunger that took her by surprise. They'd made love twice today and she still wanted him with an intensity that took her breath away.

When she pulled back for air, she smiled at him. 'I'm not doing it lying down in the snow, whatever you say.'

'Shall we go back to the lounger?' His eyes were dark with desire, the café noir tones melting into inky blackness, his voice husky.

'Okay.'

With less shrieking this time round, Holly stepped quickly through the snow and then sank into the bliss of the hot Jacuzzi before swimming over to the indoor complex.

She hardly remembered she was naked. She felt sexy. That had to be a first. Perhaps these thermal springs were magical after all.

***

He was in deeper than he'd planned. Scott couldn't believe he'd been so carried away he could've continued right there in the pool without the condoms that were still in his jeans pocket.

Holly was special and all the more so because she didn't seem to know it. He could stroke her soft curves all day long, look into her eyes and enjoy the connection he found there. He thought he'd be able to talk to her, when it felt right, about what had happened to his sister and the awful low he'd hit after her death.

In other words he had it bad.

They made love slowly, stroking, kissing and fondling each other with an intensity that made it hard for him to hold back. He postponed his climax with difficulty, so he could make sure she'd been tipped over the edge into orgasm.

Then she straddled him, wavy auburn hair cascading over her shoulders onto her pale, rosy-tipped breasts. She looked directly into his eyes all the while. Finally he believed those words about two becoming one. He'd had plenty of sex before. He'd even had sex that meant something.

But he'd never had sex like this.

He suspected it was new territory for her too. It was too early to talk about this being serious but while he might not be ready to verbalise it, he knew without a doubt something special was happening.

Later he fetched the white robes and slippers left in the cloak-room for them and took her upstairs to the Thermal centre café, not yet opened.

'Would you like some champagne?' He led her to a clear glass table that had been decorated with a multitude of tea-lights.

'Yes please.' She sat down at the table, her hair falling in wild waves around her shoulders; her face flushed a rosy pink.

He poured a glass of champagne for her and a glass of mineral water for himself.

'Aren't you drinking?' she asked.

He could lie and say it was because he was driving. They were extremely strict about drivers' blood alcohol levels in Switzerland.

But how could he even contemplate lying after what he'd said to her?

'Actually Holly, there's something I need to tell you.' He sighed. Of course he couldn't lie. He needed to be straight with her, even though this was heavy stuff for what was essentially a first date.

'Let me guess, you're not drinking because you're pregnant?' She laughed. When he didn't smile, a marked apprehension crept into her eyes and he thought it was like clouds blotting out the sunshine.

Yep, he had it bad.

'Something terrible happened to my family a while ago, a year ago in fact, and it all got rather… well, horrific is the only word that really describes it.' Scott sighed.

'Oh?' Holly's face paled and she seemed suddenly fragile in her oversize-toweling robe. Her reaction surprised him, although it was sweet of her to be so concerned.

'I didn't cope very well. I started drinking heavily as a way of coping and it got out of hand so…' He broke off she got clumsily to her feet, scraping her chair back roughly as though she couldn't wait to put some distance between them.

'What's wrong?' he asked, perplexed. He couldn't understand her white face, couldn't understand why she was looking at him like that, as though he'd betrayed her.

Accusation shone in her green eyes and he felt as shocked as though she'd slapped him.

'I can't do this Scott. I just can't.' Her hands trembled. 'Please take me back to the chalet now? I'm going to get my clothes.'

She wouldn't meet his eye but stared at the floor as she spoke. 'Sorry, I really mean it. I'm sorry, but I've got to go.'

Then she turned and fled down the stairs in her eagerness to get away from him.

CHAPTER SIX

Bile rose in Holly's throat. She felt sick to her bones, far worse than she had earlier in the helicopter. It was so bad she thought she might literally throw up on the side of the road or in the footwell of Scott's Landrover if he didn't stop to let her out.

The grim set of Scott's jaw and the taut silence between them increased her misery. She'd hurt him badly, she knew she had. The air crackled with unspoken anger and recriminations.

What more do you expect? He spills his guts to you and you cut him off mid sentence and run away from him?

You're lucky he's giving you a lift home.

Scott didn't say a word for the entire drive back to Chalet Repos. She spent the journey trying hard not to cry and concentrating on not being sick as her stomach churned and bitter bile rose up in her throat.

There was no way round this. She couldn't do it.

She would never do it. Dating an alcoholic was her greatest personal taboo. It was perhaps the only criteria that would automatically scratch any guy off of her potentials list.

Even if they were as drop dead gorgeous as Scott.

Potentials list, huh! She was lying to herself if she was going to pretend Scott meant no more to her than her previous boyfriends or crushes.

If it's the right decision why do I feel so wretched?

With great effort she held back the tears pressing heavily at her eyelids by squeezing her eyes shut.

'Goodnight.' She tried to get Scott's attention as they turned separate ways in the Chalet Repos corridor.

'Goodnight.'

She shrank bank from the bitterness in his tone. There was a blank hardness to his expression that chilled her. Not only had he put the shutters down between them but he'd brought out the barbed wire and guard dogs too.

'I'm sorry Scott,' she apologised again to his retreating back but he didn't turn in her direction or give any indication he'd heard.

Choking back a sob, Holly rushed to the bathroom, the only place she could lock the door and make a call in private. Sinking down to the floor, back against the door, she pulled out her phone and dialled.

'Hi.' Pippa's voice was sleepy.

'Sorry, did I wake you?' Holly tried to speak quietly so no one else in the chalet would hear her. Silent tears cascaded down her cheeks unchecked. It was as though she had taken her finger out of the hole in a dam and now there was nothing to stop the flood.

'What's up?'

Thank God Pippa knew her. Thank God. Holly sobbed aloud then, a gut wrenching, animal type sob escaped despite her desperate attempts to keep it in.

'Holly, talk to me, what's wrong?'

'I, I... I met someone,' Holly choked out.

'That's a good start. So what's the problem then, is he married? Has another girlfriend?'

'No, no, it's nothing like that.' Holly snuffled, grabbing some toilet paper to wipe her face. 'He's my boss – single, gorgeous and the best well, you know, I've ever had...'

'Err, forgive me for not being quick on the uptake but where exactly is the problem?'

'He doesn't drink.'

'Isn't that a good thing? After all you don't like heavy drinkers because of your mum.' Pippa spoke slowly, as though to someone deeply deranged.

To be fair 'deranged' was exactly how Holly felt at the moment. The hurt was utterly overwhelming. She tried to tell herself she'd hardly known him long but it didn't help.

'I mean he doesn't drink because he used to be an alcoholic.' Holly sniffed and grabbed some toilet tissue to wipe her nose.

'But he's sober now?' Pippa asked.

'Yes, but that's hardly the point.' Holly couldn't keep the irritation out of her voice. She'd been sure Pippa would understand.

'Why? Isn't it the point? Come on Holly, your mum is completely different. From what you've told me I don't think she's ever been sober, has she?'

'No.' Holly sniffed.

'So, this guy is different. He isn't drinking now which means he sorted himself out. He runs a business for goodness sake, doesn't that say something to you about how different he must be to your mum?'

'I suppose.' Holly shredded the toilet paper in her hands into tiny bits, feeling very young and adrift on the tide of an emotion with the power of a Tsunami to wreck her life. 'But what if he fell off the wagon? I just can't go through it, I refuse to go through it again, Pips.'

'I totally understand hun.' Pippa's tone was less brusque now. 'But almost anything *might* happen. You could meet a guy tomorrow who seems perfectly sober but turns to drugs, or drink or other women when he faces some life tragedy. Anyone *might* drink Holly.'

'Maybe.' Holly drew her knees up to her chest, hugging her legs. The sense of what Pippa was saying seeped into her mind but her emotions lagged way behind, too immersed in the knee jerk reaction they'd instigated.

'Look at it like this,' Pippa urged. 'What you hate about your mum is that she never tries to help herself and doesn't want to. He's clearly the opposite of that and has beaten his demons with alcohol as far as we know. Do you even know if he was a full-blown alcoholic? Did he tell you why he started drinking? If you understood then maybe you'd be able to cope with it better.'

'I don't think he'll ever speak to me again.' The wet tide on Holly's cheeks increased its pace again.

'Make him listen. He obviously likes you a lot to tell you in the first place. He's your boss after all, so he took a big risk confiding in you. Think about it.'

'I s'pose,' she sighed. 'I think I've messed up the best relationship I ever could have had.'

'Don't give up yet Holly, you can do this.' Pippa's tone hardened. 'It really isn't like you to fold so easily.'

Holly sighed again, a gulping, chest-heaving sigh that released a little of the tension she'd been accumulating since Scott's speech. 'Cheers Pips, you're the best. How are you feeling anyway? Any more kicks from the bump?'

'Yes, mostly at night. I think the baby's going to be a night owl.'

'I can't wait to see the baby.'

'Oh no you don't,' Pippa warned.

'Don't what?' Holly tried to make her voice sound innocent.

'You are not getting on a plane and coming back home. I won't let you.'

Rumbled.

'But Pippa…'

'I mean it. You sort things out with your boss first and then you can have a cuddle with your new godchild but not before.'

'Yes ma'am.' Holly felt the first stirrings of a smile on her face.

Thank goodness for best friends. And thank visa for the credit card she was going to have to use to pay her by now astronomical mobile phone bill!

'What?' Scott scowled at Magda who'd dared to interrupt his black thoughts by knocking at his office door.

'The clients have been asking for you.' Magda smiled, her red lipstick gleaming, obviously freshly applied for him.

Scott sighed. 'I'll come out and chat to them at supper. Can't you manage until then?'

'Of course, you can trust me to handle things,' she simpered. 'Would you like me to make sure Holly is elsewhere for supper? After all, it's clear you two are… not getting along.'

The faux concern in her voice infuriated him and he swallowed down a surge of fury. It burned in his tight chest. He'd never shouted at his staff before but there was always a first time. How dare she?

'No thank you Magda, there's no problem. Whatever's between me and Holly isn't really up for general discussion. It's private.'

'Well, if there were a problem,' she simpered silkily as though he hadn't spoken, 'and you'd like me to get rid of her, you only have to say.'

'How very kind of you.'

She didn't appear to notice his sarcasm. Perhaps her thick skin came from all those layers of make-up she wore?

A memory of Holly's glowing face, bare of all make up as she swam in the thermal pools came to mind and it was all he could do to hold onto his composure. Holly had made her position extremely clear.

He had to forget her.

'You know the offer's still there, whenever you fancy taking me up on it…' Magda smiled again and he was left in no doubt as to which offer she was referring to.

'No, I'm good thanks,' he replied tersely, his eyes narrowed. 'Now if there's nothing else?'

He turned back to his laptop and stared at the screen until he heard the door close. Then he cursed and closed the laptop with more force than was necessary. Damn, he hoped he hadn't cracked it. He stared morosely at the door, still unable to believe how stupid he'd been.

Rule one – Don't date chalet girls.
Rule two – Don't dump emotional baggage on your first date, or your second or third....

Neither of the rules was exactly difficult to remember so why had he made an exception in Holly's case? He'd never felt the need to tell his other girlfriends. In fact, before Holly he'd rather have extracted his own teeth than broach the subject.

Holly's different. She's special.

Yeah, so special she ran out on you just as you'd told her your most private secret, well tried to tell her. She didn't even hear you out…

She'd been the last person he imagined would judge him. It'd been a truly hellish time after Zoë's death. His parents had barely spoken to each other except to snipe. He'd tortured himself by remembering Zoë's pain; by wishing he'd insisted she go to the doctor sooner. He'd have dragged her along kicking and screaming if he'd known.

Hindsight was a cruel tormentor.

I could have saved her.

The old accusation wormed its way back into his mind, slithering in the dark shadows. He took a deep breath. He'd conquered this once and he could stay strong again.

I don't need alcohol. I need Holly.

Need or want? Who knew where the line lay when passion was involved? He wanted her more than he'd ever wanted anyone. He craved her easy companionship in a way he'd never craved alcohol. He'd never found the peace he felt with Holly at the bottom of a bottle.

Would he ever make love to her and laugh with her again?

'Get over it,' he growled, jaw tight and teeth clenched.

He'd never felt the need to share his life with anyone before. Work had been his main focus, particularly since Zoë's death. It had been his solace and his salvation.

Yet somehow it didn't now feel as satisfying as it once had. He thought of his plans for expansion into Italy but they just didn't excite him today. He'd have to work even harder until it did the trick again. He lifted his laptop lid and opened his email.

***

Holly chopped carrots, trying to concentrate on not cutting any of her fingers off and to not think about the wave of nausea threatening to make her retch. It was her turn to do supper tonight and Magda was doing dessert.

Hmm, I wonder if Magda's discovered the little surprise Steve's prepared for her?

She couldn't imagine being able to swallow a single mouthful of the casserole she was preparing. There'd been a low level queasiness in her stomach ever since the night with Scott at the Thermal baths.

Sharing a room with the others had made it impossible to hide her misery. Sophie had been sympathetic, Amelia less so, and Magda had been unable to hide the smug triumph dressed up in her own particular brand of pseudo-sympathy.

Holly hadn't told them much, but they all knew she'd been out with Scott for the evening and everyone had noticed they were barely talking or looking at each other since then. If Magda had been able to resist crowing to Amelia about how she'd arranged for Holly's Facebook account to be hacked she might have got off… Luckily for Holly, Magda's shrill tones carried a lot further than she realised.

She'd considered going home. The situation wasn't providing a nice holiday atmosphere for the guests after all. But she hadn't saved up enough for a flat deposit back home yet, not for London rental prices anyway.

Yet the thought of going back to London and never seeing Scott again had been unbearable. She'd tentatively tried to talk to Scott a couple of times but the fierce scowl that seemed to be a permanent fixture on his face lately had withered her words almost before they'd left her lips.

She had to put an end to it tonight, one way or the other. She'd dealt with Magda and now it was time to sort things out with Scott. After supper she'd go to him and apologise properly. It'd been rude of her to run out on him when he'd gone to so much trouble. She would explain why her response had been so… dramatic and see where things went from there.

The knife she was using slipped and she narrowly missed cutting her thumb.

Concentrate, Holly!

It was impossible. Scott had taken up so much space in her head she should be charging him rent. The memory of him inside her haunted her dreams at night. That was when she was able to sleep. It was mostly impossible. Especially when she thought about how physically close he was, how easy it would be to slip down the corridor and climb into his bed. He was just a few rooms down the corridor in his own suite. The wooden chalet walls seemed flimsy and ineffective barriers to keep them apart.

Yet she'd been unable to find the courage. Tonight she would do it. She would seduce him and wrap her apology up in kisses.

We should be together.

She tipped the carrots into the bowl and pre-heated the oven. Pippa had been right. Holly had thought a lot about what she'd said. Scott was nothing like her mother. The way he'd treated her with consideration and well… dare she say love, was a far cry from the sporadic and utterly unreliable drunken affection she'd received from her mother.

She'd left home behind years ago, or thought she had, but now it appeared she was still carrying it around with her. What better way to exorcise the ghost than to be brave and take a chance on Scott?

71

Once the casserole was safely in the oven she went to sort through her clothes. She'd look nice tonight if it killed her. She'd wear her one and only killer dress – a bright red silk wrap dress she'd got in the sales. It draped over her curves in a very flattering way, even if she said so herself. She would also wear her best underwear and shave her legs.

It was time the seduction tables were turned on Scott.

***

Scott was roused from his office by the persistent bleeping of the smoke alarm. Great. Another problem he could do without.

When he reached the kitchen, clouds of smoke billowed from the oven. He quickly flicked the dials off, briefly registering the temperature was on full whack. Then he flung the terrace doors wide open. The air that rushed in was freezing cold but at least it was fresh. Grabbing a mop from the cleaning cupboard, he used it to reach up to stop the smoke alarm beeping.

He turned when he saw a flash of red dress at the periphery of his vision. It was Holly. Wearing a red silk dress that clung to her curves so snugly it actually made him jealous.

He'd never been jealous of a dress before! Hadn't she been on supper duty tonight? Why was she all dolled up? The thought she might be planning to go out and meet someone later tonight hit him with the force of a heavy cudgel.

Anger growled in his chest at the thought of anyone else touching Holly.

'Where on earth were you?' he snapped, dimly aware that his anger was all out of proportion to the burnt supper but unable to control it.

'Just in the bathroom,' she said, biting her lip as she went over to the oven to examine her casserole 'What happened?'

'The temperature was turned right up to maximum.'

The confusion on her face turned to outrage. 'But who turned the temperature gauge up? It was supposed to be slow cooking on a low heat. And what are we going to do about feeding them? It's almost seven.' She looked at the charred remains of her chicken casserole. 'I'm really sorry, Scott. I don't know what can have happened. Well, nothing I can prove anyway.'

Magda briefly flashed into Scott's mind. Great, he was becoming as paranoid as Holly. She'd probably just knocked the dial herself.

'I'll have to make plans.' He reached into his back pocket for his phone, scrolling though his contacts. 'I suppose I can always get some skidoos brought over and we'll go up to a mountain cantine. It'll be a nice change for the guests.'

'Are we… all going out?'

'Well, you need to eat, don't you?' he replied belligerently. 'Unless you've got other plans for the evening?'

He looked her outfit up and down. She blushed.

He was being a sod. He knew he was, but it was bloody hard being in such close proximity to her all the time. So close and yet not able to touch…

Magda burst into the kitchen, smirking, her heels clacking on the wooden floorboards. 'Is everything okay in here, Scott? Can I do anything to help? Has Holly ruined the supper?'

The look she flicked across at Holly was vicious, pure vitriol.

'Someone turned the oven temperature up to maximum. Probably someone who was in the kitchen after me… you know, maybe it was you Magda?' Holly's eyes blazed with barely controlled fury.

He watched Magda's face, saw the pure hatred flash in her eyes. Suddenly he'd had enough.

'Magda, I'd like you to pack your bags and leave.' He broke in and for a moment he wasn't sure who was the most shocked out of the three of them. He didn't care about the possible repercussions. Legally he probably didn't have a leg to stand on but he didn't care. Any amount of money to get rid of her would be worth it. He had to rid Holly of Magda's poisonous presence.

For a moment Magda just gaped. 'I'm sorry, you're taking the word of the girl you've been shagging? How predictable.'

'You can have two weeks wages but I don't want to see you around here again, got it?' His jaw clenched with the effort of controlling his temper.

'Right,' Magda spat her words out, 'I'll be on my way, clear out so you two can get cosy again shall I? I hope you enjoyed your Facebook fame, Holly?'

'That's okay Magda.' Holly held Magda's gaze. 'I'm assuming you haven't checked your email yet today? Someone forwarded me your Match.com profile and it looked... rather interesting.'

Magda stared at her for a minute, frowning and then stalked out of the room. If looks could kill, she'd be stuffing both their bodies into bin bags right now.

Match.com?

He'd have to take a look and see what Holly was on about.

'Can you tell the others what we're doing Holly? I need to make some calls.'

He strode out of the room. God knew what else he might do in this mood. Him, Holly and that red dress alone together in one room was *not* a good idea. He had to remember nothing had changed. She'd made it clear enough hadn't she?

He noticed she kept the dress on when they were all ready to leave later. She'd just slipped on her boots and coat and hitched her dress up to get onto the skidoo. He made sure he went on a different skidoo. He wasn't sure he could trust himself in that close proximity to her.

The mountain cantine was inaccessible by car; the winding mountain roads were impassable once the snows came. The snow grew ever deeper as they drove up the track. They passed fir trees were heavily laden with snow and frozen waterfalls that looked as though they'd been suspended in time.

The guests seemed to be enjoying the ride. Sophie and Amelia giggled when the snow spray hit them, they didn't seem to be missing Magda all that much. He'd never understand the complexities of female friendship. But Scott couldn't enter into the atmosphere. He had no small talk to offer.

Perhaps he should go to Italy for a bit and put some physical distance between him and Holly. It seemed ironic that this time round it'd been him who'd read too much into the affair, him who was having trouble letting go.

The mountain cantine was a traditional chalet, roof laden with at least a metre of snow and icicles. Inside, however, the fire roared in the open hearth and heated the room so effectively they were soon peeling off layers. Hurricane lamps on every wooden table added to the cosy atmosphere.

Holly collected the ski jackets, scarves and gloves from the guests and made a pile by the hat stand. She tried to catch his eye but he deliberately looked away. It was childish he knew, but the things he wanted to say to her had no place here in the restaurant.

'Scott, please,' she whispered, throwing a nervous look back over her shoulder to see if the others were listening.

Something in those eyes stopped him from turning away from her. She looked close to tears and the vulnerability reminded him momentarily of Zoë. For one moment he felt that to be horrible to her was in some strange way to be horrible to Zoë.

If Zoë were here she'd probably be kicking him and giving him a shove in Holly's direction. His sister would have liked her, he felt sure they would have been friends. That was if they'd ever had the chance to meet.

'What?' He took off his ski jacket.

'Can we talk later, when we get back?'

'I thought you weren't interested in talking. You made that rather clear.'

She winced. 'I'm sorry, I deserve that. Please let me explain, just hear me out and then, then... if you want me to leave Chalet Repos I'll go, because this can't go on.' She jerked her head back to the table where it was obvious the girls and some of the guests were straining to hear their conversation.

She was right.

But how could he let her leave?

'Okay, we'll talk later, if only because I'm dying to know what you did to Magda on Match.com.'

She smiled back at him, her face relaxing a little.

He strode quickly back to the table before his emotions could get the better of him. 'So, who's for raclette? Or fondue? Or if you're really not into cheese then they do a good Rosti here.'

He glanced up at Holly who moved reluctantly from the hat stand back to the table. What could she possibly have to say that would make what happened the other evening okay? He could have been childish and refused to listen to her, just as she'd refused to listen to him. But he could see in her eyes she was genuinely sorry. There was no indifference there, only a pain that echoed his own.

CHAPTER SEVEN

'I'm a gold digging bitch but I look pretty hot, so if you go for the obvious, slutty look...'

Scott laughed out loud at the screenshot of a match.com profile bearing Magda's photograph.

'I don't even want to know how you did that, I'm hoping she can't trace it to you?'

Holly shook her head, the corners of her mouth twitching. 'I'll get Steve to take it down tomorrow. I just needed her to know she couldn't mess with me.'

'I think you managed that okay. I'm also thinking I need to stay on the right side of you.' He handed back her iPhone and as their fingers touched he started, as though burned.

He withdrew his hand and moved back behind his desk. 'So, you wanted to talk?'

Holly took a deep breath and smoothed the silk fabric of her dress down over her hips. 'Talk, yes.'

Time to be honest.

Scott leant back in his chair, looking the picture of indifference. Only the slight tic of a muscle in his neck told her he was feeling… anything right now.

That tic reassured her, made her swallow down her fear. Scott was human and it was up to her to make things right.

She cleared her throat. 'I'm sorry I didn't give you a chance to explain, Scott. If it's any consolation I've been feeling really awful about it. I'd like to explain why I ran off like that, if you'll give me the chance?'

From the furrow that appeared on his forehead she guessed he was biting back the urge to refuse. The desk was too much of a barrier. She walked towards him and round the table so he was close. Close enough to touch.

She leant back against the edge of the desk, her chest felt uncomfortably tight. Maybe it was best to just come out with it.

'My mum's an alcoholic.' She stared down at her shoes. 'When I left home I swore I'd never put myself through… living with that again. I don't think I could bear it, to be with you and it all be great then, then…'

He reached out and laid one of his hands over hers, squeezing gently. It gave her confidence to carry on speaking. 'So, I know that doesn't excuse running out on you and being so rude but I hope it explains it?'

She risked looking up from her shoes to his face. She saw only concern, not judgment. 'You do understand I panicked, don't you? It was my crap that caused it. It wasn't even really about you.'

'I do understand and I'd never do anything to hurt you.' His hand gripped hers even tighter. 'My sister died Holly, and for a while, everything was so awful I chose whisky to help me through. Luckily I realised what was happening to me before I got too far down that road and I managed to kick it into touch before it destroyed me.'

'I'm really sorry to hear about your sister.' She edged closer to him, resting her free hand on his forearm. 'I do understand. I'm not being judgmental, really I'm not. I just…'

It was impossible to phrase what she was feeling, words were inadequate to express the host of emotions jostling for headspace.

'I could never imagine choosing alcohol over you Holly.'

'Oh.' She blinked hard, refusing to start crying now.

He stared straight into her eyes. It occurred to her they hadn't looked directly at each other since that night. Not properly.

Now they had, she knew the connection between them had never been severed. The magnetic tug was still as powerful as ever.

An overwhelming desire to make love to him consumed her. She tried to remember what she'd planned to say to seduce him. Well, she had nothing to lose. She took a deep breath.

'You know Scott, I was wondering, don't you ever feel the need to let go? To give up control to someone else even if it's just for a ten minutes?'

Staring at his face it wasn't too difficult to read him. Dilated pupils had turned his dark eyes to sparkling granite. Her lines, reminding him of another time in this office, the first time they'd kissed, had hit home.

'Let me take control now, here in this office and when you go back out you can take the control right back again. If you want to that is...'

She gently trailed her hand up his inner thigh and squeezed it before reaching for the ties of her wrap dress. She took his silence for acquiescence, letting her dress fall open and exposing her best underwear. Then she shrugged the dress from her shoulders, letting it fall to the floor.

She had his attention.

'Let me say sorry for running out on you.' She knelt in front of him.

The only sound in the room was his rapid breathing, a sound that grew louder when she unbuckled his belt and unbuttoned his jeans. When she released him he was already hard. As she took him in her mouth his deep groan told her he liked what she was doing.

He knotted his fingers in her hair as if trying to anchor himself to her and sighed deeply as she caressed him with her tongue. Once he felt ready for her she took out the condom she'd secreted in her bra, placing it on the desk.

He laughed. 'What else do you hide inside your clothes? A spare bra, a condom…'

'Shut up and kiss me,' she ordered. Their lips met hungrily and Scott grabbed her rear, pulling her onto his lap.

She straddled him, edging further up his lap so the silk between her legs provided a flimsy barrier between them.

She'd planned to tease Scott a little but she was wet for him already. Touching him had turned her on and not being rejected had lead to a euphoric relief. She arched her back, thrusting her breasts towards him, gasping with relief and desire when he reached out to cup them in his hands.

Groaning aloud, Scott pulled her closer still. His lips were everywhere, kissing her neck, her mouth, and her hair... She barely noticed when he unfastened her bra but soon realised when he took one of her nipples in his mouth.

He sucked, nipped, teased and stroked... soon her slow seduction routine was forgotten. They couldn't get enough of each other quickly enough. Frantically they tugged each other closer, yanking at clothing, caressing flesh and kissing as though they might never kiss again.

Scott lifted Holly up onto the edge of the desk and buried his head between her legs. There was more urgency this time. He tasted her with an intense and thrilling hunger. It was less playful than before but more passionate and the pleasure sharper.

Then he flipped her round and bent her over the desk, his hands parting her thighs wide, sliding up her legs and inside her, teasing her and preparing her. The leather desktop felt deliciously chilled against her breasts, a direct contrast to the heat of her sex. She wanted him now more than she'd ever wanted anything.

She waited, feeling a sharp twinge of fear that he was about to walk away, to pay her back for what she'd done to him. At last she heard the sound of the foil packet ripping. Squirming, she longed for him to enter her, was still gasping with the force of the passion that had hijacked her seduction routine.

She wasn't in control. Scott wasn't in control. A force more powerful than either of them held sway.

It was passion, a wild desire, love... perhaps all three combined. They had unwittingly ignited it and now it had them in its grip.

He entered her from behind, the angle far deeper than when he was on top. She welcomed him, gripping him tightly as his hands slid around to stroke between her legs. He caressed her with his fingers at the same time as he thrust rhythmically from behind, reducing her to a quivering mess. She was pliable, soft clay to his touch and at that moment she was utterly, utterly his.

She cried out aloud, unable to stop herself as the sensations inside her mirrored what he was doing to her most sensitive flesh. An orgasm unlike any she'd had before ripped through her, leaving her breathless and shell-shocked.

As she contracted around him he stiffened and shuddered, gasping aloud. Relief flooded her again.

He still wants me.

Of course he wanted her, that had kind of been obvious, hadn't it? And yet she was still relieved. Now that he'd come inside her she felt that they were united again.

'Shall we go to bed and talk some more?' Scott picked her dress up from the floor, looking less composed, less guarded than usual. It was as though what just happened had stripped away another layer between them, lessening the need for defences.

'That sounds good. Oh my God.' She put her hand over her mouth. 'I've just realised we forgot to lock the door!' She grabbed her dress from him and tied it around her body. 'Well I suppose we had other things on our minds.'

***

Scott felt infinitely relieved. It all made sense now. Holly had explained more about her mum and how hard it'd been for her growing up and he'd understood. In fact he guessed she'd barely told him a fraction of how bad it had been. In return he'd been at pains to answer all her questions about his problems with alcohol with complete honesty.

'I'm really sorry to hear about Zoë,' Holly had wrapped her arms around him, hugging her with her body when he'd told her all the details.

Then they'd made love again, less frantically but no less passionately.

Now Holly showered in the ensuite while Scott tried to locate her clothing for the second time. He knew something had happened between them that would change his life.

As he finally located her bra, her iPhone beeped on his bedside table where it lay charging. She'd insisted having it nearby as she was waiting to hear when her friend went into labour.

'Can you check that for me Scott? See if it's Steve?' Holly called from the bathroom. 'He said he'd text me if Pippa went into hospital,'

Scott looked at the text message visible on her screen –

Snagged that millionaire yet? ;-)

A chill spread through his body and he sat down on the bed. His mind raced, then he took a deep breath and decided to think rationally. Instinct, intuition call it what you will, he'd decided it was time to start trusting it. After all if he'd trusted it in the beginning he could have saved them both a lot of hassle.

He knew Holly wasn't a gold digger. He knew it as certainly as he could categorically state the opposite was true about Magda.

This text was nothing more than a joke, nothing to get worked up about.

If Holly had taught him anything it was to be a little less quick to judge, to go with his heart and his gut more. Life wasn't black and white. No one was infallible, himself included.

'Well, what does it say?' She popped her head around the door from the ensuite into the bedroom.

'It says 'snagged that millionaire yet?' Winky face.' He raised an ironic eyebrow and winked to illustrate the point.

Holly burst out laughing, 'God, she's obsessed. That's terrible! And the funny thing is she's with a penniless apprentice and very happy too. You'd think she'd stop trying to sort my life out.'

Her open manner made him very glad he hadn't accused her of anything. The old Scott would probably have gone away and brooded over it.

'Have you found my knickers yet?' She disappeared back into the ensuite. 'You still haven't given me back the pair you took on New Year's Eve!'

'So, you've uncovered my master plan to have you chained knickerless to the cooker then?' he called back, forgetting to keep his voice down.

That would give Amelia and Sophie a lot to talk about. Although they'd given them a fair bit already. He didn't care. He didn't mind who knew he was with Holly. It was time to realise when he'd got a damn good thing.

**

Catcalls and whistling filled the air of the packed Wonderbar and this time Holly joined in the clamour. As did all the Verbier chalet girls and female bar staff who'd squeezed into the crush, determined not to miss tonight for anything.

'Off, off, off,' they chanted.

Some of the guys looked uncomfortable, others were smirking, confident in their ski-toned physique. Scott mouthed the word 'help' at Holly but she just grinned back. It served them right. She didn't feel even a smidgeon of pity for them.

One by one they took off their shirts and sweaters while the female onlookers wolf-whistled at the toned torsos, made firm and taut by long days on the slopes.

A few show-offs stripped completely and then streaked round the bar but Holly found she didn't feel embarrassed or awkward as she might once have done.

She merely raised an eyebrow as though pretending to be

scandalised and walked over to Scott. Throwing her arms around him she claimed him as her own before some other girl took a fancy to him. She buried her face against his bare chest, inhaling her favourite aftershave with a little murmur of pleasure. She didn't think she'd ever get tired of his smell, or of being allowed to touch his chest.

The bar manager looked a little dazed as he calculated how many free shots he'd have to give away tonight.

'Equal opportunities,' Sophie shouted over to him and he scurried away. He probably thought he'd be lynched by the female contingent if he didn't comply.

The mood they were in, it was quite possible. Girl power was temporarily in force and they planned to enjoy it while it lasted.

'I'm surprised you didn't hide another T-shirt underneath your shirt,' Holly murmured into his ear.

'I thought about it. I could break your cover, you know. Tell them you didn't hand over your own bra. They'd make you do it again.'

'Just you dare!' She poked him in the ribs.

'Ouch.' He wrapped both his arms around her, holding her close. 'Don't worry. I want you all to myself. You can do a strip for me later tonight as a forfeit.'

'Okay.' She laughed.

'Are you having fun?'

'Yes, I'm having fun.' And for once she didn't wish for a snowdrift to swallow her up. 'Do you think I'm a proper chalet girl now?'

'No, you're a Holly,' he said, holding her in a tight embrace. 'Refreshingly unique and lovely just as you are. I don't ever want you to change.'

Then he kissed her and it felt like they were the only two people in the room, despite the crush.

'So, you're going to stay with me after the ski season ends then Holly?' He presented it more as a statement of fact than a question. 'Switzerland is beautiful in the spring and we can go mountain biking. Didn't you put mountain biking as an interest on your CV?'

She playfully swatted him on the arm. 'No, I did not. And I want to make full disclosure that I haven't ridden a bike since I was eight! But I'm happy to give it a go. Both the staying on and the mountain biking.'

And she was.

Blissfully and unreservedly happy. She knew real life would throw some rocks in front of their skis from time to time but she was sure they'd manage to negotiate them.

Instead of having her nose pressed up against the glass of the cake shop window she was now very much inside and licking her lips as she ate the stickiest bun in the place.

'Come back to the chalet with me, I've a rather urgent matter we need to attend to,' Scott murmured in her ear, his breath prickling the skin on her neck.

'I know. I can feel the urgent matter against my hip.' She grinned, surreptitiously lowering her hand to brush against him.

Scott groaned, stiffening against her hand. 'You evil woman.'

'You brought me over to the dark side, it's your own fault,' she teased.

'I've created a monster.' He pulled a horrified face. She poked him in the ribs again.

'Get a room you two,' Sophie called out good-naturedly.

'Good idea.' Scott slipped his shirt back on, manoeuvring them out of the crush of bodies to where they'd left their jackets.

Soon they were inhaling the tranquil night air and walking through the snow that sparkled in the moonlight.

'You don't have any more confessions for me, do you Holly?' Scott asked, his eyes inscrutable.

'Yes.' She stopped walking and stared at him seriously, only waiting long enough for the first worry line to appear on Scott's face before she put him out of his misery.

'I need to confess that I think I might love you,' she said quietly, her heart hammering in her chest.

Scott's eyes blazed with heat as he pulled her close and kissed her, slow and delicious.

'I think I might love you too, Holly Buchanan, slalom queen, chalet girl and burner of casseroles…'

'That wasn't me,' she interrupted. 'You know that wasn't me.'

He went on as though she hadn't spoken. 'But, all things considered I think I'd like to keep you on. I have another position I'd like you to try out. Well several in fact.' He grinned wickedly and Holly flushed again, her cheeks hot.

Damn it, would she never stop blushing around Scott?

On reflection she hoped he never stopped making her blush.

'That's an interesting proposal Mr. Hamilton. Perhaps you'd like to go over it in more detail?'

'It would be my pleasure.' He clasped her hand. 'It might take some time though.'

'That's okay, I'm not going anywhere.' An unfamiliar peace settled over Holly as they entered Chalet Repos.

I feel like I've come home.

The house was aptly named – it was a refuge, a place of peace for her.

She knew she'd finally come home to a place she hadn't even dreamt had been waiting for her. Life was what you made it and she was going to make it a good one.

'Okay?' Scott asked, pulling her towards him and tugging impatiently at her buttons.

'You know Scott?' She smiled, a smile that felt like it was stretching from ear to ear. 'I think I am, I'm really okay.'

She slid her arms around his neck and kissed him. She'd been given a chance and she was going to take it.

Fancy seeing what the rest of the Chalet girls are getting up to? Look out for more books in this deliciously naughty series!